Praise for Colin O'Sullivan

"A hard, poignant novel of great humanity ... remarkably well written ..."

—Rolling Stone (France)

"O'Sullivan's voice—unique, strong, startlingly expressive—both comes from and adds to Ireland's long and lovely literary lineage. Like many of that island's sons and daughters, O'Sullivan sends language out on a gleeful spree, exuberant, defiant, ever-ready for a party. Only a soul of stone could resist joining in."

—Niall Griffiths

"His words swagger with purpose, never meandering too long on a scene, always moving the story forward, even when it goes back in time, like a faded photograph coming into view. Lyrical to a point, one word flowing to the next, hardly stopping. I read this novel and saw a movie in my mind – that's how each page appeared to me – and that's a good thing. This story reminded me of a beautiful vase, now shattered to pieces on the floor. But with each piece picked up and glued back into place, a narrative came into being, with each piece representing a character, beautifully written with all their flaws and realism, broken by their own imperfections and weaknesses. But most of all, the dropping of the vase, once beautiful, representing by the act of a man, long gone, though his actions reverberate through the years, waiting, waiting for those sunny days in Killarney, when the sun finally gets to shine on that long buried seed, giving it the energy it needs to bloom – for good, and for evil."

—*Love, Sex & Other Dirty Words*

"A cathartic novel that ultimately creates positive emotions, like the blues can do. Poignant."

—*Book Node*

"A luminous novel that chases away the darkness … All its characters are at a crossroads and they will either meet the Devil himself or find a way towards a new life."

—*Appuyez sur la touche lecture*

"Carried by a genuine writing talent, *Killarney Blues* is a Noir novel full of melancholy and unfulfilled dreams with a surprising glimmer of hope at the end. Without the slightest naivety. A revelation."

—*Le Soir* (Belgium)

"*Killarney Blues* is a Noir novel – but not only – at the farthest reaches of love, desire and loss."

—*Lettres d'Irlande et d'Ailleurs*

"A novel of great finesse and humanity. Perhaps, sometimes, there is a glimmer of hope in the blues?"

—*Action-suspence.com* (Starred review)

"In a style that is sometimes luminous, sometimes direct, sometimes poetic, Colin O'Sullivan traces his narrative path, creates incredibly vivid and appealing characters and brings the reader, to the 12-bar beat of the blues, towards a heart-breaking denouement."

—*Le blog du Polar de Velda*

"This first Noir novel from Colin O'Sullivan is magnificent, very finely written, and profoundly sad. To be savoured while drinking a Guinness and listening to some old blues, by Muddy Waters or Bessie Smith. And if rain knocks on the window glass, like in Killarney, it's even better."

—*RTL (Radio Télévision Luxembourg)*

"Moving, tragic, masterly crafted."

—Lea Touch

"*The Dark Manual* is a mature rounded work, assured and confident, at times lyrical and beautiful but also punchy and sharp. […] engaging, inventive and thought-provoking."

—*NewBooks.com*

"Colin O'Sullivan is a lyrical master of the written word. There are sections of the book that are heart-breaking, in their emotional and physical sense of loss, and moments of humor, surprise, suspense, pure sudden horror, and stark naked joy."

—Marvin Minkler, *Modern First Editions*

Marshmallows

~~A play~~

A novel

by

COLIN O'SULLIVAN

BETIMES BOOKS

First published in the English language in Dublin, Ireland, in 2020
by Betimes Books CLG

www.betimesbooks.com

ISBN 978-1-9161565-4-8

Marshmallows is a work of fiction. Names, characters, places, and incidents
are either the product of the author's imagination or are used fictitiously. Any
resemblance to actual persons, living or dead, events, or locales is entirely
coincidental.

Cover image © Ichy Sriwongthai, with his gracious permission

Cover design by JT Lindroos

For Patrick O'Sullivan

Vladimir: You were afraid of the whip?

Boy: Yes Sir.

Vladimir: The roars?

Boy: Yes Sir.

Vladimir: The two big men.

Boy: Yes Sir.

Vladimir: Do you know them?

Boy: No Sir.

Vladimir: Are you a native of these parts? (Silence.) Do you belong to these parts?

Boy: Yes Sir.

Estragon: That's all a pack of lies. (Shaking the Boy by the arm.) Tell us the truth!

—Samuel Beckett, *Waiting for Godot*

"Does it please you when you walk onto a stage and everybody looks up and watches you? Maybe they don't want to watch you at all. Maybe they'd prefer to watch someone else."

Harold Pinter, *The Dwarfs*

Table of Contents

ACT I

I

A white van drives along quiet suburban streets. The forecasters say that snow is unlikely, a touch of sleet at most in the evenings perhaps, but no White Christmas for those romantics hoping and praying for a sprinkle of magic. There will be nothing like that here, no chance.

The only white thing visible on this night is this van motoring along, going through the gears, looking like it has to be somewhere and something important to do; the Christmas season is all rush, and this vehicle could be its embodiment, so full of purpose it is as it speeds and pulls recklessly into the forecourt of a closed petrol station.

The driver does not wear a Santa hat; instead it's a black balaclava. His eyes in the rear-view mirror are narrow in focus, a man not only with a job to carry out but intent on doing it quickly, and calling no attention to himself or his vehicle. Perhaps he should've taken out one of their other vans – his twin has a black one too, everything about them doubles up – but here he is, white van man, and he looks busy, he doesn't waste any time, never does.

He takes a hammer out from the bag on the passenger seat. He parks, climbs out, leaves the engine running, while he sprints to the front of the shop. There are signs on the windows there – messages about scrumptious sandwiches, delicious snacks and bouquets of fresh flowers, half-price boxes of chocolates; a list of classifieds too, people are always on the lookout for something, eyes for bargains, or for something to offload. But he has no time to make out these letters in the dark, no time to consider the deals on offer, he has not even stopped for petrol, the pumps are closed at this late hour, no one there to attend – he has only one job this first night, only one simple task, and he aims to do it fast and then get right back.

He finds the security camera he is looking for but realises that it is a little too high on the wall for him to reach. He is a big man. He is a very tall, well-built man – years at the gym has made him taut and tough, obsessive body-building, pounding down the protein drinks; he's fearless in all he attempts – but this camera is just that little bit out of reach. He pulls a wheelie bin over to it, climbs on top and breaks the lens of the camera with one swift and accurate blow of his ball-peen hammer. He jumps off the bin and rolls it back into its original position.

Sweat gathers inside his balaclava and he wants to take it off and wipe his eyes. But he can't. There's no time for that now. No mistakes. Get in, get out. These were the orders he was given and Brick is a man who never disobeys his orders. It has always been this way for him: you do what you're told and you do it well. He is the quiet type. Just like his brother. Identical. They were quiet in the womb and they came out quiet, hardly making a sound – one midwife remarking on the eerie silence, as if they had all stepped into a momentary void. What was there to cry about? Why moan? The brothers just get on with things. They leave the plans to those who are better at that kind of thing, leave it to the dreamers, the schemers. This man, Brick, he knows his strengths: speed and agility, power, and the never getting caught. This the most important of all: the never getting caught.

He skips around the outside of the premises looking for other cameras that he may have missed on recent reconnaissance. There is one attached to the side of a petrol stand in the main court and he quickly gets to it. This camera is well within reach and he smashes it expertly with a hard emphatic swing. Minute bits of plastic and glass fall to the ground and crack under the soles of his big boots and he spins around to see if anyone has seen or heard. Not a soul. Nothing stirs. It's the middle of the night – or early morning, depending on your take. The only sound is his own heavy breathing inside this hot mask, and the sooner he can pull it off and let the night air assuage him, the better.

He sprints back to the white van, flings his hammer in the direction of his bag and drives hurriedly out onto the street, lucky to have no other car passing, lucky to have no one witnessing anything at all.

He finally gets to remove the itchy balaclava, the material rasping against his stubble as he does so, and he breathes deep and satisfyingly, his skin already cooling in the December air that blows through his open window.

The van speeds through the holiday-decorated wintry streets, and he catches sight of one overhead street hanging: it's a big, neon plastic Santa Claus and the words: *Ho Ho Ho.*

Indeed.

Ho Ho fucking Ho.

It is hard not to agree when things go according to plan.

2

Ben Morrigan is writing on thin strips of paper. He is sitting at the table and has an array of things spread out in front of him: pens, glue, scissors, Sellotape. He got up early this morning because he doesn't want to be distracted. Ben Morrigan is the kind of man that doesn't like to be distracted from whatever it is that he has set his mind to. Christmas means nothing to him. Christmas is nothing *but* distractions, coming at you from all angles: from shops, from TV, from your phone. He is tired already of the Christmas enthusiasts, their fake smiles, their well-wishes, their crass cards and clumsy carols, ironic sweaters and mass consumption.

This Christmas will be different.

Plans afoot.

It is about time that he took control of the situation once and for all. This is the season, if not of *good*will, then just *sheer* will. The will to finally make it happen. To finally put an end to it. After all these years. The time has come.

He had the dreams again the night before. They keep on coming, rarely stopping for more than a week or two. A savage drooling dog that never stops barking, whips and ropes and trees that stretch up into the sky and never seem to end – anxiety dreams, this is the stuff he has to deal with, crippling, choking, devastating dreams. There is always the possibility of a giant at the top of one of those trees – or are they beanstalks? – but just as you climb to the top and poke your head through to see what's lurking above the clouds ... nothing. Nothing at all. Nothing emerges. There is ever only the idea of a giant. The threat of a giant. Its massive thudding steps on the boards shaking the whole house, shaking the whole world, shaking Ben's bed of course and Ben *in* his bed, having him jerk awake and gasp as if punched full-on in the gut. A giant punch and a giant gasp. This is how he wakes. Several times a month. There's nothing he can do about them.

And it's always the same faces there. The same instruments of torture. The same gruff, cavernous voices.

Time for giving and receiving.

He wakes in sweats.

He wakes in tears.

But he's always damn glad he actually wakes.

Waking is relief. Relief is eyes wide open and staring at a blank ceiling and nothing at all going on. The sight of nothing.

Relief is the sight and sound of nothing. Or the sound of his own breath calming down. Slowing, regular, easy does it.

Someday he might sleep in peace. Someday maybe sweeter dreams. Or better still, the bliss of none at all, no memory coming back to him. Nothing from his past, nothing to haunt. A perfect blankness.

These little blank pieces of paper now in front of him need to be filled in. He needs to write his instructions down. He writes neatly so that no one will be in any doubt as to his intentions. It is no time for sloppy handwriting, he's got to make things abundantly clear: they should be under no illusions.

This is the way it is to be.

His way.

Glue, paper, scissors, pens, markers, tape: he's good with all this stuff, good at making things, he's always been like this, and then there's his level of concentration, so focused, deep, deep concentration when he puts his mind to something. *Do not disturb.* It could be a sign hung around his neck.

David ambles into the kitchen, his usual lackadaisical gait, never in any rush, unless he's getting ready for a night on the tiles, when a kind of antic euphoria overtakes him. He's Ben's boyfriend and they couldn't be further apart in their personality traits.

David, however, isn't his usual amiable self, not on this particular morning, because a hangover is getting the better of him. He's tugging at his curls as enters the kitchen, as if the hangover might somehow seep out through the hair follicles and disappear through his fingers and out into the ether. *Away, away, begone you demons!* But no such luck. No magic here.

He sees his partner at the table, busy with one of his projects. There is nothing unusual about finding Ben here, in the morning, or any time of the day, planning, scheming, constructing, that deep concentration, always deep.

"I didn't hear you get up," David says, the echo and effort of his own words already hurting his head.

"Didn't want to wake you," Ben says, though without much warmth.

David fills the electric kettle, his actions slow and cumbersome. He looks at the cloudy water rushing from the tap. He was told never to trust the water in London – it's nowhere near as clean as what he grew up with in Dorset – but isn't the act of boiling going to purify it, isn't that what is supposed to happen? He is too tired and weak to argue with himself, too weak to rationalise or remember anything from his secondary-school years and the science classes he was supposed to have been paying attention to. Only seven or eight years ago, those schooldays, but already they feel like a lifetime has passed. He had felt trapped then. The small country school. The famous actor for a father, theatre legend and occasional daytime TV star. But he's more than made up for the village years, was quick to put the constraints of the country behind him, and he enjoys the high life of London still, frequenting the best clubs, the hottest, hippest bars – sooner or later he will stop and grow up, surely that's his plan ... just not yet, a few more months perhaps before he gets his arse into gear and proposes to Ben and attempts to make a proper go of it.

He will ...

Just needs to straighten himself out first.

Soon, soon.

He will.

David makes promises to himself. He makes New Year's Resolutions. And boyfriend Ben will need to snap out of his moodiness too, whatever winter blues he's got himself entangled in. He yawns as he prepares the kettle, all his actions slow and cheerless on this mopey morning.

Ben tries to ignore the sight of him and wrinkles his nose as if something very unpleasant has fouled up the kitchen, breaking his immense concentration. He might be able to tune out from the *sight* of David, but he's finding it hard to ignore the whiffs of last night's pub crawl coming from his partner's hair and fetid breath, from last night's pub *and club* crawl, which Ben, typically, sagaciously, gave a wide berth.

David turns to look at his boyfriend but Ben has his head lowered again to the accoutrements festooned across the table, his brow furrowed and his dark eyes wide with interest – he has, as ever, the intense focus of a bomb-maker.

David switches the kettle on and opens a new jar of instant coffee, punching a hole on the top covering with his finger. The popping sound of his finger through the gold covering pleases his not-yet-fully-with-it sensibilities, and he allows himself a smile, the sound reminding him of the previous night's blatant debauchery and someone popping a bottle of champagne. He remembers the heaving nightclub, David doing his best to look louche at the side of the dancefloor, cavorting with a group of male revellers (and leering at plenty others), hugging, laughing, and incessantly moving to the dense rhythms, the inescapable beats.

They held out their champagne flutes greedily while a handsome man – Brendan, he said his name was, or was it *Ronan*? – poured the bubbly which frothed and spilled to their resounding cheers. Merry. Very Merry Christmas. Indeed.

He will not tell Ben about any of this.

He never does.

What Ben doesn't know...

Not that David would ever cheat on him or anything like that; he does really want to give this relationship a go. But Ben has been so preoccupied of late, and never comes out to any social event. It was different when they first met. Ben seemed far more active. Active and attractive:

the long hair he used to let hang around his shoulders – only recently shorn – the overall sense of buoyancy, all that seems to have disappeared. Ben had been eager to impress David, both of them actually took turns to woo and be wooed, but since moving in to David's flat Ben has become dull, the whole thing, the relationship is becoming rather stale – one of David's friends even joked that they were like an old married couple already; David will have to do some serious soul-searching if he wants to make it all work. This Christmas should be a good test of things. A meeting with the parents. A visit to his father's home. The big deal of Christmas: family time, celebration time, if that doesn't bring them closer together then … he'll just have to … well, he'll have to think about all that later. He is not about to let it ruin the festive season. Not now. Resolutions. Later. He'll make them. Soon, he will, soon.

David takes two mugs off the rack, one a plain blue, the other with Star Wars written in its famous thick black slanted font above the picture of a Stormtrooper. Ben said the mug was childish, ribbing David for hanging onto his past – Ben will do almost anything to forget his. A plain blue mug will do just fine for Ben Morrigan, he doesn't need anything advertised. He likes things plain. He wants to be a simple man, a simple man with simple plans and his time … it's nearly upon him.

David slides a teaspoon into one of the mugs and it rattles.

Ben looks up, casts one of his looks.

"Instant? Really?"

"I can't be bothered, mate. Anyway, I think we're out of filters."

"We're not out of filters. You're just too lazy."

"I'm too hungover is what I am. This season already taking its toll."

David doesn't need to look at the calendar. He knows it's Christmas Eve. Calendars, clocks, photographs, they are all too brutal in their honesty. It's different when you are out at night and dressed to the nines, full of booze and banter in your best boots. And he doesn't want to see how carefully Ben crosses off each day with a red marker – God forbid that it ever get done in black; David has encouraged his partner to see a therapist, if not for the terrible nightmares, then at least for the OCD-ish tendencies, the pedantic pushes for things that are of no consequence … and Ben in turn always encourages David to just go and *fuck right off.*

Perhaps David's friend was right, they *are* like an old married couple already.

"You're such a socialite. Can't even keep track of the days. It's all just one big party, isn't it?" Ben can't conceal the hostility in what was supposed to be delivered with levity.

David doesn't pick up on any of this, doesn't know if he is being reprimanded or called to give an account of himself. He has hardly even woken up.

"Don't knock parties. It was at that Halloween party last year we met, remember? You looked so terrifying in that mask. Like something from a Francis Bacon painting."

Ben doesn't respond. It was good, that mask, grotesque. What's wrong with scaring the shit out of people every now and again?

"I'm getting too old for it all anyway," says David.

Ben lifts his head from his work, "You're twenty-five for fuck's sake!"

David does what he often does in situations like this, he ramps up the camp.

"I know darling … and feeling every minute of it."

There is such flounce in the delivery, it is sure to get on Ben's wick, which is probably its intent.

Ben shakes his head, he has fallen for it. Rankled. Even further now.

David goes to switch on the radio; perhaps he can lighten the mood, give himself something that will take his mind off his horrible headache.

But Ben is quick to flare.

"Don't!"

"Why not?"

"Because we might get Cliff Shitard, or Shakin' Stevens or that fucking awful Paul McCartney one."

"Sorry," says David, "such a dangerous time of the year. It's so easy to ruffle your feathers."

It often goes like this, David apologizing for something insignificant, and feeling uncomfortable now too, even in his own home, if not downright alarmed, the sudden rages of Ben, they seem to come out of nowhere – one moment you are in the middle of a normal conversation and the next it is as if a wild bird has been let loose in the enclosed space, its wings beating frantically about your head.

The kettle has not yet boiled and David fiddles impatiently with the electrical cord at the back of it, causing it to spark.

"This fucking thing. We need a new one."

The kettle putters and purrs back to life and David forces himself to be positive, a full-on argument now will do nothing at all to alleviate his heinous hangover.

"What are you doing there anyway?"

"Making Christmas crackers."

"Making?"

David has seen him make many things in the past. Ben's job after all is to make props for the sets of stage plays, TV shows, sometimes even movies. He is endlessly creative, good with a whole host of materials, but making your own Christmas crackers – who the fuck would bother? Who the fuck would be so cheap?

"Since I'm meeting your parents for the first time, I thought I should make an impression."

David softens.

"That's so sweet. But homemade crackers, really? We're not that hard-up, are we?"

Ben bristles at the "we", can never seem to get used to it. He was more used to being solitary, being abandoned, more used to fending for himself. But he is in a relationship now, and he needs to see it all through.

"I bought the set online. Actually they're turning out quite well."

Ben holds up a shiny red and green cracker, the quintessence of Christmas: the shiny green, the deep and fulsome red – you could imagine a whole host of Santa Claus' elves applauding the colour combo and its perfect shape.

"Impressive. You really are the craftsman, aren't you?"

"My job."

"I know darling, I…"

A sudden flush comes to Ben's face, his temper about to burst yet again.

"Enough with the *darlings*. I don't want you to do any of that in front of your parents. It's fucking embarrassing."

Not for the first time in their year-long stint together a tense silence ensues. Sometimes their characters simply clash. It is inevitable. The short, curly, friendly, all-dancing extrovert with the moody, brooding, tall, dark and secretive soul. David's friends ponder the mystery of how they fell for each other in the first place. But Ben had used his moodiness to his advantage then, in the meet-cute early days, his introverted nature somehow magnetic, pulling in those around him, daring them to try and unveil, to try to crack his code. Some friends were convinced that was the crux of the allure, while others doubted he was even gay at all – *just didn't look it.*

They are still together, however. The quickest year of their lives. And tense silences may simply become the norm. They have never come to blows. Voices are never raised … or never all that much.

These mini-episodes are usually extinguished before they ever really catch fire. David has grown accustomed to Ben's grumpiness. Ben is like that when he's focused, preferring the peace and quiet of working solo. Although he only moved in a few months ago, he has already taken over the spare room like it is his own personal artist's studio, with theatre and movie junk everywhere: props, masks, toys, replica items, guns – which shocked David when he first saw them, they looked so real. David has never been to the company Ben works for – Ben assures him it's just a pokey little workshop – and he fears this flat could quite soon be a pokey little workshop, too, if more tools and toys and tricks continue to accrue.

The click of the kettle finally turning off snaps David out of his fug. He spoons instant coffee from the jar into the two mugs, and pours the hot water into each.

"And you have some lame jokes to go into the crackers too?"

"Jokes, no. Instead they're more like … instructions."

"Instructions?"

"Yes. Like … what you have to do."

"Do?"

David places the plain blue mug in front of his boyfriend. From behind he gives Ben's shoulder a squeeze and rubs the back of his head and neck. David preferred the long, thick locks his boyfriend used to sport, now the tiny hairs are coarse and rough, as if this is the head not of an artist at all but of a soldier, about to be fitted for a helmet, about to go to war.

Ben doesn't exactly recoil but he looks like he'd prefer to stay working on his project. Would prefer solitude, silence.

David looks down at the array of craft-making equipment and stationery items. He's waiting for Ben to continue his explanation. With Ben you had to give him time – his temper is quick to flare, sure, but not his explanations, his accounts of himself, his reasons, or any heartfelt opinions, they're all slow in coming.

Ben makes David wait.

Sometimes you simply had to do that. You had to simply wait. For plans to come together. For things to start making sense.

3

As Charles Cunningham stands in his large living room waiting for his son and guest to arrive, he regards his decorated tree with a great deal of studiousness. He's had over six decades of different Christmas trees and they have grown even larger and more ornate. This one though, there is something fundamentally wrong with this one... even if he can't quite put his finger on it.

His wife Lydia is perched on their leather sofa in an elegant blue and white dress (especially purchased for this day). She has been looking forward to seeing her son – it's been ages, and to finally meet his boyfriend will be an honour. She is delighted at being allowed in on David's life; never really knowing what he gets up to in the city, and it is perhaps best she doesn't, well aware that her baby boy has a reputation for being a party guy – Charles had to be quite stern on several occasions, in the early college years with money and time going down the drain. But surely he's outgrown all that. A mother can only hope. He still has that thesis to complete, and she doesn't want Charles to get all riled up because of it. She'll just have to trust her son to make the right decisions, and trust too in the man he brings home this day.

She leafs through one of the Sunday supplements to pass the time. It's one of those magazines that has nothing but pictures in it, hardly anything of substance to read, but she scans it anyway, hoping there might be some titbit on a trending food, some useful information on the right recipe for the right occasion, maybe even something about Greek food – she really should research more about it, at least a quick Internet search, they're going tomorrow. Tomorrow!

Her husband disrupts her idle thoughts.

"Does this look lopsided to you?"

"What?"

"The tree. Does it slant a bit to the right? Or is it just me?"

"I think the whole room slants a little to be honest. It was built all wrong. Not quite flat."

"Don't be daft."

"Seriously. I noticed it the first time we moved in."

"You've never once said, not in the million years we've been married."

Lydia laughs in her usual gurgling way. It is one of the things he still finds most attractive about her; she still has the impudent laugh of a naughty teen.

"A million years," she says. "Funny, it seems like a lot more."

Charles moves closer to the troublesome tree. If he attempts to reposition it he'll only make it worse. His wife is better at those kinds of things, the putting up or the taking down. She'd have a shelf on the wall and perfectly straight before Charles would even have found his toolbox. *Her* toolbox. Charles would hardly be able to name half the things inside of it.

"Stop footering around," she snips.

"*Footering?*"

"Fussing over nothing. Being annoying. I know you're nervous but look... look, no one will notice if the tree is slightly... askew."

"*Askew. Footering.* I've always loved your turns of phrase. I'd never come up with those."

"That's because you're an actor and it's not required of you. You're just paid to mouth what's already written down for you. No originality."

He chuckles, "You're probably right."

"If you've lived the life of a bored housewife you'd know that you have to be creative all the time."

Charles folds his arms, knows this is gearing up to be as long as any stage monologue. She was born into a loquacious Scottish family, what she says herself were a hard breed never short of an opinion or two. He loved to let her at it, expounding on whatever was the topic of the hour. He watches her now, laying aside her Sunday Style magazine and letting loose.

"When you go to the supermarket and have to see the same faces day in day out, you have to be a bit creative in each encounter. You can't keep saying the same old stuff to the same people all the time. There are only so many times you can say: *How's the lumbago, Mrs. Clifton?* without driving yourself, and probably Mrs. Clifton, insane. You've got to come up with new greetings, new smart remarks, new witticisms. And because half these old biddies are on Tweeter, they are all used to saying pithy things, and saying them wittily. Even the auld ones, even the ones as old as ourselves. It's quite the arena, I can tell you. Of course the latest, I mean, over the past few weeks is: *Are you all set for Christmas?* Which gets bandied about quite a lot by the less creative. I love the *all set* bit, as if a great preparation is necessary, or a great race. It's priceless really, the discourse, and hard to keep a straight face with them sometimes."

Charles is smiling at her. It means he can take a break from worrying about that Christmas tree and whether it will topple over at any minute. She continues:

"And I'm sure there will be women up and down the country also saying the same thing tomorrow morning: *I'd better go check on the turkey.* As if the bloody thing was going to kick its way out of the oven and run away, headless down the road with stuffing coming out of its arse."

Her husband lets out a great guffaw, "Not only the vocabulary, but great imagery there too, my dear."

Their days go like this. Sometimes they are at loggerheads. Oftentimes too they are in hilarity *at* one another, often *with* one another. They are well aware of the absurdity of marriage, of society, the craziness of the world they inhabit. They are educated people, and they have lived some years.

Lydia rises from the sofa and puts the magazine on the coffee table in front of her. She yawns and stretches.

"I better go check on the bloody turkey."

"You better hold off on the *bloodys* and *arses* when the boys arrive. Don't want to let the side down with that coarse Scottish tongue…"

She cuts him off before he can get any further, hands on her hips and sticking out her considerable chest.

"I don't intend censoring my language for anyone, sweetheart. Anyhow, that boy, he grew up in some kind of care home or something, so I'm sure he's heard some choice language over the years, and seen a thing or two in his time. You don't know what those poor boys have been subjected to."

A look of sudden sorrow comes over Charles.

Lydia sees his frown, those bushy eyebrows turned inward.

"But he's made good for himself, apparently. Good with his hands I hear. David says he's very resourceful."

"Yes, resourceful. I heard that," says Charles. But his mind has gone elsewhere. Those poor boys ... subjected ... for a moment the room really does feel like it is aslant, and the master of the house is a little unbalanced – he hasn't had a drop to drink yet, but the room, the room feels like it suddenly reels.

4

Ben is twisting the paper end of a Christmas cracker into position when a grim fantasy comes to him.

Imagine if these cracker ends were actually necks; imagine they were the necks of David's bourgeois champagne friends, their thin hipster necks hiding behind their long hipster beards; imagine my hands around those necks, gripping, wringing, strangling, breaking; imagine the popping sound of hipster bones breaking, breaking…

"Well?"

"Well, what?" says Ben, wanting to wade more in his delicious daydream.

"Instructions…you said. What you *have to do*. What do you mean?"

Ben looks at the Christmas cracker again, the colourful items laid out before him; for a second he's lost and trying to find his bearing.

"Right. Well…it's like…one paper might say *put on a party hat* or *stand up and recite a line of poetry*. That kind of thing."

Improvise, Ben, improvise.

David sits at the opposite side of the table and takes a sip of his coffee.

"Like a parlour game. I see. Father will have a field day with that. He likes those kinds of games. Anything that involves, you know, theatrics."

David does his best to mimic his father's deep voice: "One of the finest actors ever to grace the boards of London, or any stage anywhere."

Ben looks at him, alarmed:

"Are those his own actual words?"

"Some critic said them somewhere once, a lifetime ago, and Father has been trotting them out ever since. I wouldn't be surprised if he'll have them engraved on his headstone. I'm not sure how true it is. I mean, I don't know who actually said it. But he seems to believe it. Maybe that's the reason he's been successful. Confidence. Mum just rolls her eyes … and has another drink."

David takes another sip of coffee and tries to make like it tastes all right, but he is making a poor fist of it. He should have searched for those filters, should have done it properly – Ben was right.

"They're heading to Greece tomorrow, winter break, lucky sods. That's the reason for the turkey today. We've always had it on the twenty-fifth … and he's a stickler for tradition."

Ben takes a sip from his cup now, wincing at the taste. It's not that Ben has ideas above his station, nor is it that he is in awe of the middle classes. It's just he believes that certain things should be done in a certain way, even if the process takes that little bit longer. Society has become concerned with speed, with immediacy; sometimes the best things in life take a little longer. *Instant* rarely the answer.

"Hasn't he retired?"

"He still takes *old man* roles if they come up. Though I'm pretty sure he wouldn't like me saying that. He did Spooner a few months ago in that Pinter play ... can't remember the name of it now."

"*No Man's Land.*"

"Of course, you'd know. Mister Props Guy."

"Keeps you in beers," says Ben.

David playfully puts his hand to his heart as if he has been pierced, but Ben is not laughing, he hadn't meant it as a joke. He still does not look at David directly, he keeps his head down. Is it the fact that David stinks from the night before, that the pongs of bar and club linger in his every pore and are pushing out from him now and colliding with the air molecules of this spotlessly clean kitchen? Or is it that Ben knows that David had flirted shamelessly with all and sundry the previous evening, regardless of gender, or of sexual preference – it has happened several times before, embarrassing Ben, it was embarrassing really, out of order, show a bit of decorum for Christ's sake.

"I've acted a few times too, you know. When I was young. Amateur stuff. But a few proper productions."

Every so often Ben shines a little light on his past. The light is usually a weak, battery-dying-faint-torch-glow, not a klieg light finding an escaping prisoner in a cinematic epic ... but still, something, and David will gladly take it.

"You've never said before."

"I played the boy in *Waiting for Godot* once. It's funny that we're doing a production of it again now, I mean ... as a designer now of course. The tree ..."

Ben's words trail off, immediately regretting the pride he had briefly allowed himself. He doesn't like to give too much away. When he was growing up in the orphanage it was quite the opposite, trying to completely sell himself when a couple came round, like he was a cute dog kept unfairly in the kennels. You had to put on your best smile, seem all eager, seem normal, seem like you would not cause any trouble at all no matter where you were sent – you had to give the impression that you most definitely would never ever shit on their carpet. All this had to be impressed upon them with eyes. Sad eyes. Hangdog eyes. But you had to maintain that lively smile. It was hard to get it right, hard to find that balance. The nervousness always seemed to be pulling the facial features in different directions. Ben forever failed. Acting was not his thing after all – he is better behind the scenes.

When the lights were on him back then, no matter how nervous he had felt, he was able to get his lines out, recited them perfectly on the stage. He can still see the costumes of the entire cast: the rags, the bowlers, Lucky's snow-white hair cascading out from under his hat, Estragon's trousers falling down, the jokes, the japes. These come in the dreadful dreams too, all these images, echoes still sounding in the dark recesses of night. The foster family had given him permission to be there; the orphanage too had said that it would be OK; the boy had good looks, a certain charm about him, might be useful on the stage, it's not like he was missing any school; the nuns would get time with him, make sure he caught up with his lessons again. The nuns made sure of everything.

"But doesn't the boy in Godot only have a few lines?"

"More than a few, actually," says Ben. "Mostly short, though. Mostly *yes, Sir, no, Sir, I don't know, Sir*."

Ben can almost hear the crack of the tyrant's whip across the stage floor.

What is he rattling on about? Why is he even telling David about this? Stop, Ben, stop.

Nothing should be revealed now, nothing is to be gained by this – if anything, it could put all his plans in jeopardy, derail everything.

"Go on, say some more. Say some of the boy's lines," David urges, his morning suddenly brightening.

Ben stares at the Christmas crackers, needing a way out, feeling uncomfortable. Why did he even mention ...

"No, I ..."

"Go on. Whatever you can remember."

Ben tries a half-smile, embarrassed, all this of his own making of course. He should never talk about his past, never mention the things he's done. He should keep his mouth shut. It is the only way to get on in this world, let the lairy arseholes makes fools of themselves with their Twitterstorms and tabloid tantrums. Cunts.

David's face is nothing but encouragement now, his eyes two pleas.

Ben clears his throat. He is, stupidly, a bag of nerves. Fuck it, do it, be done with it:

"*Mr. Godot told me to tell you he won't come this evening but surely tomorrow.*"

David claps and hoots, like it is some sort of breakthrough, or like he is a fawning father himself and his boy has just wowed on stage in front of scores. *Britain's Got Talent. The Voice.*

"Father would be proud," he says.

Ben shudders, as if some icy thing has run down his spine – he is not yet ready to deal with David's father. He needs a few more hours to fully prepare.

David watches Ben packing the crackers carefully into a box and wrapping it with expert delicacy. He becomes focused again. Calm and concentrating. Bomb-maker fixation.

"Don't forget the ribbon," says David.

"I always wrap things up nicely," says Ben, knowing his sentence carries more weight than David will ever know.

He is focused again. He is making Christmas crackers which he bought online. He is good with his hands. Resourceful. Creative. This is who he is. This is who he is.

He tries one more sip of the coffee, "I'm sorry, mate. Can't finish this. It's horrendous."

This is also who he is ... if things aren't done properly ...

"Sorry, my tongue doesn't know any better," says David. "The punishment I put it through last night. That pub was such a dive. I'm never going there again. And the nightclub wasn't much fun, not without you."

Ben knows this is all bullshit, but he'll let it slide. He'll deal with all that later.

David of course did have a lot of fun without his moody partner. He remembers gyrating on the dance floor, getting close to a number of equally enthusiastic revellers. He could smell their sweat, the alcohol on their breath, he can smell it yet.

One dancer – Brendan, Ronan? – spoke loudly into David's hand-cupped ear: *come back to my hotel.* It was more imperative than invitation. David had to shout back over the thumping music that he was *taken*, and that Ben would be sure to find out, Ben just seemed to have ... *ways*.

The sexy Irish clubber was not about to give up so easily. He was only in town for the weekend. He pleaded with David to let the brute go, that he'd have a lot more fun with him. His words rang to the rhythms of the music:

Come back to mine. Come back to mine. Come back to mine.

But David remained steadfast. He held his ground on the slippery dance floor, telling him that he couldn't, that he was – and here was the deal-sealer: *ensnared in love!* He had even used those words – or maybe the copious amount of champagne had said them for him – how fucking shameful it was now thinking back on it! Such a stupid fucking thing to say: *ensnared in love!* Jesus Christ!

Irish Brendan or Irish Ronan had told him quite matter-of-factly that Ben sounded like a right arsehole, whether David was *ensnared* or not, and he'd be sure to regret it.

David found it difficult to disagree, and ended their encounter with a what-can-you-do gesture, then just drifted away, not knowing – in the game he had just played – whether he had won or had been defeated.

"You should give it all up. Stay sober. Stay focused. Get fit. Try *Dry January* at least."

Ben is dishing out advice in clipped, staccato bursts, but it sounds more like an admonition.

David looks down at himself, pinches the inch of flab that has sprouted in his mid-section – it's not quite *pot belly* yet, but it's belly enough to make him blush.

"Just like you, you mean. My perfect man. Full of willpower. Tower of strength."

Ben is not certain if what David says is sincere or just a subtle plea for forgiveness after the careless carousing of the night before; perhaps it was a lame attempt at morning seduction – for all David's hangover bleariness there is a glint in his eye.

Ben is doing his best to ignore his partner, but when David leans back on his chair and his dressing gown opens to reveal a bare and hairy leg, he can only scowl.

"You should shower. Get dressed."

"Yes, boss."

David points to the Christmas cracker Ben is examining with almost forensic studiousness.

"Are those things going to snap when pulled?"

Ben refuses to break his concentration; it serves as a massive hint for David to go and leave him alone, give him some peace. He should never have been forced to quote those lines, those Godot lines from when he was...that poor boy...   •

"Anything will snap if you pull it hard enough," he mumbles, jest-less.

David feels a shiver go up his spine. Is it the damp of the wintry morning outside, or is it Ben's dusky demeanour – David doesn't mind admitting he often feels brief flurries of panic, as if Ben possesses wells of danger yet untapped.

He rises from the table, goes to the sink and plops in his empty mug. Perhaps Ben was right about that much at least: the Star Wars mug did look a little on the childish side; maybe it was time to ditch such things. You'd have expected Ben to be the movie buff, but the toys and the replica items, the masks and guns, they were all for work and work only, as he is always quick to explicate. Ben has laid his childhood to rest; he's all about adulthood now, proper behaviour, the right way to go about things. They really are opposites. How had this relationship ever come about?

You two are like an old married couple already.

David shakes himself awake and turns to face his day.

"Right, shower first, then we get ready for the road. They're going to be so excited to see us. I'm sure Mom is basting the turkey right now. And there'll be Brussels sprouts, too. Imagine that."

"I don't think I've ever even had those," says Ben.

"What? Really? Well then you're in for a treat. They're hardly exotic. You'll be farting for hours after."

He ties the belt of his robe tighter around himself, his burgeoning belly and hairy legs now fully concealed.

"And if Mum does us some of her special Yorkshire puddings..." David is nattering to himself as he leaves the room.

For a moment Ben closes his eyes. He had hardly slept the night before. Nightmares again. An imposing, dull grey building. Nuns in their black garb waddling like crows and pecking at young boys for the things they did or the things they didn't; a small long-haired boy, knock-kneed and nervous, dragged along by a hard hand, practically getting his arm pulled from its socket. A black Rottweiler lies on the ground, writhing in agony, it cannot get something out of its mouth, it is choking, not enough air reaching into its lungs, it convulses, perhaps it does not know how to breathe through its nose, or the chain, the chain is pulling on its neck, choking; a hard Irish sport that one, *hurling*, one of the Catholic nuns insisted: *will make men out of you unfortunate bastards* – she would wield a stick herself, wielded it like she knew exactly what to do with it, like she could smash the very shins of Hercules.

Brussels sprouts? He hadn't even known what those were. Meals had been even more simple, appearing before them on hard tables, from what they had grown in the walled garden: carrots, potatoes, parsnips, onions; the meals could have come from a Dickens tale, the morning gruel they swore was porridge, but who could say for sure what it contained – no one would have believed it was the mid-1990s, it felt like a throwback to an older, cruder time, and the few remaining nuns were adamant it stayed that way, it was a tough world – you might as well be prepared for it. They were a dying breed, those short women and their bowed black heads. Ben had thought the whole world was dying back then, and that the end of that particular decade would surely be the final nail on it all, a new millennium was surely only a pipe dream – but here he is, beyond it all now. The world did not end. And here he is, still in it, trying to take control of at least a part of it.

The last image that comes to him is that of two taller boys by his side, sandwiching him, and him feeling somehow safe there, the safest part of that trinity. Things were good right there, pillared on either side. Nothing could touch him.

His eyelids snap open like roller blinds. He drags himself out of his chimera.

That's better. Much better. The *now*. Things to do. Things to be getting on with. No point dwelling on the past. There is so much to do.

He gets up from the table and pours his shit coffee down the sink. He washes his mug along with David's, dries them both and returns them to their rack.

He switches on the radio but after hearing only a few seconds of Slade's "Merry Christmas Everybody" he turns it off, shaking his head dismissively, as if it is all personal, this world against him, everywhere an enemy.

He leans back against the sink, folding his arms and taking in his surroundings. He's been here a while now, this flat, the months flown by as he dreamed and schemed ... but this place is not his home. No place ever is. Except maybe in the middle of two tall others, sandwiched and safe. Pillars. Power.

He scowls again. His face is like the weather outside the kitchen window now, descending to inclemency, sour.

5

Charles sits down on the sofa and stretches out his long legs. He is still looking at the Christmas tree and wondering whether he has gotten it all wrong this year. He should have left it to Lydia; she would have made a much better job of it, it wouldn't look unbalanced the way it does, so unstable. But he had insisted. He had wanted to do it himself, to feel useful, to help around the house. Now that parts in plays were becoming fewer (and in decline for several years) he has more time on his hands, and he doesn't want to saddle her with all the domestic duties, even if it is quite clear that she is far more accomplished in running an orderly household.

Lydia has indeed checked on the turkey – her anxiety at the imminent arrivals starting to kick in. All morning she has tried to relax, tried to keep her mind off it, but it hasn't quite worked out that way – the magazines and newspapers cannot keep her interest, Charles is getting on her nerves and … she probably just needs a stiff drink.

"Are we all packed up?" he asks, looking up at her with as much innocence as he can muster, and quite admiring too of the cut of the dress she is wearing for the first time.

She had gone ahead and booked the trip herself because, although he had promised it for her birthday in October, he had completely forgotten all about it when the time came.

Worrying moments like this have only increased of late: memory lapses, finding himself in a room but completely at a loss as to what task he was to perform there. Twice she had to put the bins out herself, which is one of his only chores. So he finds himself failing. He is letting her down.

His father had gone quickly, one minute on the golf course, fit as a fiddle, the next: didn't know what decade he was living in, seemed to reside in some ethereal past.

"Of course we are ready," she tells him. "When have I ever *not* been ready for travel?"

They try to go abroad at least once a year and have been to Amsterdam, Paris, Barcelona, Rome, Florence and their favourite, Prague, twice. It was Greece's turn this time and the islands there, because Lydia is dying for even a sliver of sun, summer had been unnaturally cold and wet and even Scottish people can only take so much. Surely even Greece would have a bit of warmth in winter.

"Only … I can't find my notes," he says.

She needs to stay calm, but she needs to be tough with him too, let him know the way she is feeling.

"You're supposed to be retiring. The reason for going to Corfu is so you can wind down and forget all that. It takes too much out of you now, Charles."

She says his name softly, with a rising inflection, the intention to placate, but her husband is not giving up on it.

"It's just that there's a possibility …"

"There always is, isn't there? A possibility."

"*King Lear*," he says. "They're casting in January."

Lydia looks at him blankly, they've been down this road before.

"I just made a few notes in an old battered copy, that's all," he says. "Have you seen it?"

"No," she replies. "But if you can't remember where you put things, how the heck are you to remember lines of Shakespeare?"

"I'm the right age for it... Lear."

"You're the right type for losing your bloody mind. If I don't lose mine first. I thought we'd be able to kick back and relax. Look, you've done your work, love. God knows but I've sat through enough boring plays in my time."

She goes to the drinks cabinet and takes out a bottle of sherry. She looks at the label but puts it back again.

"It's too bloody early... but you know what, you know what, you'll drive me to it, seriously, you will."

Charles knows he shouldn't, but he decides to chance a cheeky jibe anyway, "You'd better go and check on the turkey."

She gives him a reproachful look as she leaves the room. She is not going to be drawn into any arguments, not on Christmas Eve. Her son and her son's boyfriend are to come to the house soon and she wants a perfect day for them. She wants it all to go smoothly. She wants peace and harmony and all the things people expect at Christmas. She could do with a bloody drink though, she's not sure how much longer she can wait.

Charles is left looking around the room, taking in all the decorations he put in place. The Christmas cards are all lined up along the mantelpiece, and he has lit those tasteful red candles that give off that lovely strawberry scent. The place doesn't look too shabby at all, not too shabby at all.

He leans his head to the side again to study his crooked Christmas tree, the only thing he hasn't gotten quite right this season. Sometimes you just make mistakes in life, simple errors, like everybody, but what about *amends,* how do you go about making those?

6

Ben walks into the bedroom and hears David singing in the adjoining bathroom. It's Mariah Carey's "All I Want for Christmas" and it is woefully off-key. Not that that has ever stopped him before. Many times has he taken to karaoke stages at work events or in Soho dives and blasted out George Michael or Robyn as if his life depended on reaching those high notes...which he never did.

But it was not for the want of trying. David is not the type to tone it down, or settle for something with a deeper lead, if it isn't high-pitched and shrieking there really is no point, thus his preponderance for '80s classics, Prince, Kate Bush. Karaoke is all about kitsch, high camp, and it looks like he is practising his pudgy arse off in that shower right now, preparing for the next time someone hands him a beery microphone.

Ben looks at the bed. A double bed. His double life. Secrets. Lies. So many conflicting thoughts speed through him right now but he's got to keep it together. There is no backing out of it at this stage. He's got to stay focused. He's made that bed.

He picks up his smartphone from the dresser and runs through his messages. He begins a reply, typing "colour?" with quick fingers and pressing "send". He looks at it impatiently but he doesn't have to wait all that long, it pings in his hand with one word: "white".

The Mariah Carey impersonation abruptly stops. Ben can hear the sound of the water being turned off and heavy wet feet stepping onto the bath mat.

Ben types back the word "naturally" in reply to his secret messenger and slips the phone into his back pocket. He's good at this. Good at secrets. He's lived with them for years.

White. They had been known to change the colours of their vehicles regularly: a new spray for a new day; plates get switched around too, it is best to ask, to know what's coming for you.

Ben is about to turn and leave the bedroom when his boyfriend emerges, a towel around his expanding waist.

"Don't run off on my account. We still have plenty time. And now that I'm all clean and refreshed, I thought we might..."

Ben looks suddenly flustered, needing an excuse to get out of there again. He is fast to improvise:

"I'm going to make some coffee. Proper stuff this time."

His boyfriend rolls his eyes, throws the towel across the bed, stands there naked and rejected. This has been happening a lot. They've hardly touched each other: Ben always making excuses, Ben always working on some assignment, always preoccupied. It hadn't been like that at the beginning, there had been warmth, there had been a modicum of affection, but it seemed like it was fading more and more. Last week David had read an online article about Seasonal Affective Disorder. Some people displayed symptoms of depression at the same time each year, usually in winter, even though they had been quite regular in mood and behaviour for the rest of the year. SAD it was commonly known as, and David could believe it. Is that it? Is Ben in the grip of some kind of mood disorder? He daren't bring it up. Not now. Ben had enough going on with the nightmares, the anxiety dreams that often leave him lying awake in the middle of the night sweating and shuddering. David would have to be really cautious with him, perhaps spring would be a better season, when there is more sunlight, when the craziness of Christmas is well and truly gone and they could get out and about more and spend proper time together like normal couples, going for walks in the park, spending afternoons in the cinema and then to those little cafes they both like down by the river.

Maybe.

He'll have to wait and see.

Resolutions: hasn't he already started to make some of those?

He has thrown his towel across the bed and he is naked in his room and maybe he should have taken that guy up on the offer last night, *come back to mine, come back to mine*, even if it had been just a drunken fling, *come back to mine...* he could have gotten away with it, *your boyfriend sounds like a right arsehole.* He could have enjoyed the whole thing, the furtiveness, the temptation of another's flesh, the giving in, the letting go.

But he hadn't.

He hadn't done any of that.

Out of a sense of loyalty to his boyfriend? Out of a sense of propriety to a man who has just walked out the door on him and ignored his bare and vulnerable body?

Idiot.

Which one?

Which one of them does David mean?

Rejection stings. But there is no sense in standing around naked on a winter morning expecting him to rush back in, because Ben won't. Because when he makes up his mind to do something, he just goes on and does it. Ben is making coffee in the kitchen, no doubt finding the proper filters in the drawer or shelf or cupboard or wherever they are supposed to be. How come Ben knows more about the layout of his flat than he does? How come Ben knows where everything is or is *supposed to be*? He is probably there right now spooning exactly the right amount in to that filter and placing it with exactitude on to that coffee maker and using the requisite amount of properly filtered water. David can picture it all without sneaking down the stairs to take a peep: the precision, the attention to detail, the not fluffing his lines, he doesn't have to go down and spy on him, after their year together, he already knows that much.

David had better just put on some clothes and forget all about it. Next time he'll have to be more forthright, *demanding* what he wants. He'll have to summon up the courage. He'll have to. Make that a resolution too. But for now, he puts on his socks and pulls them up high on his calves and puts on some tight-but-trendy underpants and distressed-but-expensive jeans...and he'll have to make a decision on which seasonal sweater to wear, the one with the big Rudolph face on the front or the one with Father Christmas on his sleigh. Reindeer or Father Christmas? He wonders how that will go down with Ben. Sometimes he just asks for trouble.

7

This beautiful little theatre, built with National Lottery money and the proud push of local community, is as good as any in the West End. Sure, it is smaller and lacking city-centre glitz, city-centre renown, but there is an intimacy about it, the decor is plush and it has an air of opulence without being too showy, which immediately sets it apart from the quaint village halls in similar suburban settings that many thought it would become when the original building first got flooded and reconstruction became entirely necessary. The floorboards had rotted away and it had suffered the added ignominy of a rat infestation, but you wouldn't think that to look at it now: its rows of scarlet seats leading down to a magnificent compact stage, and actors who have had the pleasure to perform there have quite rightly praised the terrific acoustics and the way the stage manages to be in proximity to the audience and yet somehow at a stately remove – the joke being that while the audience can see the spittle fly from the actors' mouths it doesn't quite land on their cheeks.

The outside of this building is just as impressive, a mock-Gothic façade that gives it an old-timey eerie feeling, accentuated by the fact that it is casually surrounded by tall conifers that cast it forever in shade.

Brick Herbert has a key to the place. Standing at well over six feet tall, shaven-headed, with a powerful physique and the tattoo of an open-mouthed venomous cobra down the right side of his thick neck, he is the type that people do not usually say no to, they'd hardly dare. His twin, Brac, has pretty much the same effect on folk, they get away with murder (some whispering that they both, at an earlier stage of their life, literally did). Brick Herbert has ways and means of getting his hands on all sorts of things, people will hand over anything – but this time the key was simply pressed into his palm by his instructor, who happens to be a member of the current troupe readying to perform there in spring; he just gave him a copy of the key and warned him to be vigilant when entering or exiting – Christmas means the place is empty, but you never know who's watching. The only security camera (on the front wall outside, above the main door) has already been dealt a blow of Brick's trusty ball-peen hammer.

His real name is James, and though he didn't mind at all having the namesake of an esteemed horror writer, the term *bric-a-brac* got lumped on him and his twin Richard for their wheeling and dealing skills (extraordinary given that they do not speak), their fondness of a good deal, their ability to get you what you wanted, or convince you that the crap they had on offer was sorely sought after and you simply had to have it (again, this must be somehow done with their eyes, for their mouths are most often tightly shut). Over time the elder twin's moniker got an extra "k" as appendage, and the *big as a brick shithouse* simile seemed apt enough anyway. So "Brick" it is. And brother Brac is never too far behind.

Brick is alone this evening in the beautiful theatre and he is moving a solitary and emaciated fake plastic tree to the stage. He sets it to the audience's right as he has been instructed, and he also locates a set of bowler hats, a whip and a rope that have been left backstage for him and places them near the stricken tree.

He knows nothing about plays. Never seen 'em, never read 'em. He has never heard of Samuel Beckett and the only theatrical productions he has ever witnessed are those he was involved in himself as a child – nativity plays, where he stood as a shepherd on one side of the crib as his shepherd brother stood opposite. No acting chops but symmetry, at least they could manage that. The shepherds' roles suited them perfectly because they were as silent as the robes that hung off their lanky bodies. The brothers never have anything much to say to anyone, certainly not to anyone they do not know – one visiting counsellor to the orphanage had put forward the notion of *selective mutism*, perhaps the twins had shared some mental anguish, trauma or post-traumatic stress even, but the highfalutin notion was quickly tossed aside by the Mother Superior, who quipped that they were "just two silent bastards who couldn't be arsed to talk", but she happened to be very fond of them for that very reason: if only all children could be as quiet as Richard and James.

Brick stands for a minute looking out to the empty audience remembering his brief thespian stint: the shepherd rags they dressed him in, the long staff he was told to grip, but he quickly sheds the memories and goes about his business again. For all his size he moves quietly, slipping through the glum shadows of the dark theatre. He does not even use a flashlight to illuminate the scene: years of operating when the sun sets, stealing into places where he should not be to take things he should not take have given him an almost cat-like ability to negotiate the dark.

All the while he whistles softly to himself, that Paul McCartney song he had just heard on the radio, "Wonderful Christmastime", such a change in tempo to the usual throbbing beats he plays at ear-splitting levels when working out or driving in one of his vans. He hates the fucking song but some of them just stick, don't they? Even the shittiest ones. He looks again at the tree – has he got it straight? It is hardly a tree at all, so twiggy it looks, as if it was a tree left standing after a nuclear fallout, a tree from stricken Chernobyl, or the last tree left on Earth when an alien spacecraft came and nuked everything with their laser beams; it looks like it might topple at any minute, so Brick makes sure to position it the way he was instructed, leaning a little yes, but sturdy enough – his boss, or at least the instructor of this particular operation, is a stickler for detail and has shown him the photos of the exact shape and set-up – things had to be just so, it is almost a sickness of his, and Brick, having pretty much grown up with him, never fails to disappoint; there is loyalty between them, a sense of enormous trust as well as admiration, and Brick doesn't mind being told what to do if the person telling him makes complete sense, and makes him part of a decent deal. Life is kept most simple that way.

Brick Herbert steps back to look at the stage from the audience's perspective and is pleased with his work. He sets a camera in position too. He's looking forward to what will happen here. He's never had a Christmas like this one before. It beats the shit out of sitting around at home watching whatever old nonsense comes on the telly. He is glad to be a part of it, always glad to be kept busy. He mimes taking out an invisible gun from the back pocket of his jeans and pointing it at the empty stage. He fires an invisible bullet but makes no sound at all – much as he'd like to explode with sound effect and guttural laughter, he merely smirks at his imagined accuracy and packs the invisible gun into the back waistband of his tracksuit. The theatre. What a place for it.

He starts whistling the Christmas pop song softly again as he walks through the centre aisle of the carpeted theatre, closing the door behind him and turning the key in its lock.

The words *simply, having*, echo in his mind and they're stuck there now. Shit song, but it's earwormed in. It's there to stay unless he can drag it out and stamp on it.

When he climbs into his white van and starts the engine he quickly sticks in a CD that blasts into life with raucous synths and thunderous drums.

The Christmas song has been obliterated.

Obliteration.

This is something the brothers know all about.

8

David is wearing the Rudolph sweater, complete with woollen nose that protrudes from the area around his navel – it actually sticks out. It is an unsightly item of clothing that goes beyond irony to being that of simply bad taste. It cannot be called a fashion faux pas; it is just plain wrong, humourless and hideous and should have been aborted before the first needle ever clacked against its partner.

He gets into the car, surprised that Ben hasn't yet commented upon it – if it was a strategy to annoy him it hasn't worked, if it was revenge for bedroom rejection then it has fallen flat – Ben is busy loading boxes and holdalls into the boot.

David sticks his head out the car window and shouts back to him.

"I hope you haven't forgotten your crackers."

Ben slams the car boot closed and chews the inside of his cheek, a habit he's had since childhood, a habit that lets other people know that he's mulling over something, or that whatever is simmering inside his head is more important than anything you've got to say to his face – it's arrogant, sure, but it works for him. He's not going to respond to David's attempt at a joke – he gets it now: *I hope you haven't forgotten you're crackers*, a lame kids' joke – and he never does forget his props, he never forgets anything, he stores things up, he manages, that's what Ben does, he constructs. They pull away from the kerb, away from the flat and the scene of their morning tension – just how much more would arise during a two-hour journey to the other side of the city, past the leafy suburbs and out into the countryside and the large, impressive, secluded house of Charles Cunningham, remains to be seen; but at least Ben feels like he is going somewhere, like he has something to do, a mission, set things straight, once and for all.

"Nervous?" asks David, only a few minutes of silence into their journey.

"About meeting your parents? No, why would I be? I just hope everything goes according to plan."

"Why wouldn't it?"

"Indeed."

Ben looks out the window, watching his world pass by. These aren't the streets he grew up in, these aren't his, but he's got to know them. He's always had that knack, getting to know a place quickly, becoming accustomed to its corners, its cadences. It was what he had to do when he was shuffled out the door of the orphanage and into a new abode – he'd have to size it all up, work out where the kitchen was, where the toilet was if he had to get up for a pee in the middle of the night (they weren't going to put up with you pissing the bed); how big the garden was if he was allowed to play in it; if there was a dog that might scare him or one that he'd have to shut up. This was the opposite of what he had to do on stage. On the stage he had to build a set onto the blankness, construct a something out of nothing, build from scratch, living rooms, kitchens, or the right prop to go in exactly the right place, a piece of furniture, or something an actor might pick up, might use; props are his forte, but he has been known to erect walls, often with a team of carpenters, putting up kitchens, living rooms, sheds, homes that aren't real; it isn't all that difficult, because for Ben homes are never real anyway, they are always just showplaces, just rooms where he either is or is not for certain amounts of time, places with things in them, furniture or appliances or the things people called *theirs* – the set on a stage is as real as the one between bricks and mortar. Ben had spent his youth constructing worlds and he is still at it. The places he drives past now are already set, everything is already there in stone, in metal, the hard immutable *thingness* of the world: buildings, bridges, traffic lights, signs, steadily there, whether you liked them or not. He doesn't have the same control over that kind of tangible world, it is not *his*, it is for everybody, for society, and he is unsure of his place in all that. As he chews the flesh of his inner cheek this is the thing he realises: that it is control that he wants, *his, his,* to be able to decide what goes where and for what reason, to build his own set, his own world, to design it to his specifications, to make sure things happen the way that he wants. The phrase *control freak* has been flung at him before by David in some fit of pique, but it is most probably true. *This isn't your place, Ben, the spare room is not your workshop.* When he was a child he had no control over anything, the adults ruled his world, the ones they called *grown-ups*, as if it was some kind of achievement to have gotten to a certain age, when that was only the passing of time. They told him where to go and what to do, they ruled his days, insisted on their ways, they shook their heads, *no, sorry,* when the hangdog eyes didn't work to his advantage and turned wet with tears on a lonely pillow at night, the people who swiped at his bare buttocks with a switch of birch when he got out of line. And the other children in the orphanage, each as lost and dumbfounded as the next; a collection of blank, wounded imps, abandoned, some with hope, most without, others losing it day by wretched day.

It is much better when Ben is in absolute control of the situation.

Making his things.

Setting his scene.

He is good at his job; that much has worked out all right.

Put things up. Break them down again. Make masks. Make fake things. Put things in certain positions. Good at all that. Resourceful.

David throws Ben a few sideways glances, wanting conversation, wanting him to stop looking out the window, it would surely make the journey a lot shorter.

"They'll be very excited...to see us. I'm sure of it." David is picturing kitchen bustle, preparations.

Ben can only offer something snide: "Your father is well used to our sort anyway. The theatre...you know."

David needs to keep his eyes on the road, but he can't help looking at him.

"*Our* sort? Care to expand?"

Ben doesn't take his eyes from the street. He cares not to expand one whit. He cares only for this day to go the way he wants. *His* day. Put things in certain positions. Break things down.

"Nope."

David sighs, "Then music."

"Fine. Just no radio. Stick on a CD...or something from your phone."

"What do you want?"

"Something loud."

He wants to hear something booming, something cataclysmic, something that sounds like the ground cracking and opening up below him and the damned crawling out of Hell and roaring onto this terrain; he wants something brash, bold, violent...something that sounds like heads being smashed against asphalt. That's it: heads against the hard ground, that's what he wants to hear.

David turns on the radio to spite him. He goes through the stations but nothing suits.

"I don't know why you can't get into the Christmas spirit."

"I can. I am. I just don't need to hear 'Fairytale Of New York' fifty fucking times a day."

David kills the radio.

"Let's just listen to the hum of the engine then drone all the way to the house."

"Fine."

It is actually. It is fine. Ben can think more clearly without insipid pop songs or silly DJ patter. He can think straight.

"If I fall asleep at the wheel from boredom, I'll know who to blame."

"Unless you're dead," says Ben.

"What?"

"If you fall asleep at the wheel and die in a horrific crash, you'll have no one to blame because you'll be dead. A dead man can't blame anyone."

David can follow the logic of course ... but cannot help expelling another sigh.

"Right. I can see the kind of mood you are in today. If this is because I was late coming home last night ... "

"It's not."

"Then what?"

"Nothing."

"Nothing? It seems like a lot more than nothing."

Ben leaves the sentence hang, the tension of it only expanding in the drone of the engine and filling up the tight space of the dad-bought Prius.

Ben softens his prickly stance.

"Look, maybe I am a little nervous ... that's all. I'll take over the driving in a little while if you like, we can share ... "

David agrees. He pulls out a pack of CDs from the door pocket and hands them to his partner.

Ben slips in a Birdhead CD into the car stereo system and is pleased with the heavy opening of "Custom Muscle".

David throws him another glance. He is worried about him. He is worried about the way he's been in recent weeks, worried that his own SAD diagnosis could actually be correct. He is worried about the day ahead of them too – this could all be a bloody disaster, the day, the road they are on, the figurative one more than the actual. It isn't too late to turn back on this day yet, not too late to make up an excuse. But he doesn't have the heart to disappoint his mother and father. The turkey is stewing in its own juices. Knives are being set.

He focuses on the road ahead, his part of the drive, his duty.

Ben closes his eyes and thinks of different plans entirely.

9

An open-mouthed cobra, fangs bared, forked tongue protruding: Brick rubs the tattoo at the side of his neck – Brick has got a crick. He's been bending down cleaning the gun on the coffee table in front of him, using a microfibre cloth and a cleaner (lubricant preservative), being sure to get into the nooks and crannies; his firearm will be effective no matter the environment – its style won't be cramped, not even by London's winter damp. The lack of movement while doing all this with such thoroughness has made his neck stiff and he swivels it now, trying to loosen it out. He's heard this problem called "tech-neck" on the TV, a modern phenomenon: people spend so much time hunched over laptops or looking at mobile phones that they are hurting themselves, bringing hernias upon themselves, stasis and lack of mobility might even make the very form of the human body alter over the years. Osteopathy is the area of medicine that is going to benefit from all this – that's what kids in college should be learning, how to fix sore and crooked necks, how to align spines correctly. If Brick had the brains he'd surely study that. He'd use his hard hands to twist folk back into their rightful shape. Crime doesn't pay all that much, though in fairness Brick does all right for himself. He grins to his empty flat: crooked people, it has many different meanings.

The television is on and a familiar family favourite is showing: *It's a Wonderful Life*. James Stewart probably thought it really was, not just in this movie but in his real life, he surely made enough dough from all he starred in, but Brick has no problems with the kinds of people who make money from their own talent. It is the people that keep popping up in the newspapers that disgust him, those – talented or not – who have to go and fuck with someone else along the way, or force people into positions they don't want to be in, preying on the weaker; some young lass that is trying to get her own foot in the door perhaps, or hoping for their big break.

Perverts. Ponces. Nonces. The scum abounded. Maybe things were much simpler in James Stewart's time... or maybe there were always cunts in every corner everywhere.

Brick rubs his neck again and stands up to stretch himself out even more. He picks up the assembled gun and admires its sheen, the heft of it in his hand. It cost him a pretty penny but he doesn't mind that at all, he'll always make it back. You have to invest to recoup. He keeps his business ventures simple, no stocks or shares, no paper trails, no boardrooms, no boredoms, just solid connections and old-style proper handshakes that mean something. You don't fuck with Brick, or for that matter his brother, Brac. You wouldn't dare.

He aims his spotless pistol at James Stewart as the actor runs hysterically through a snowy black-and-white town. Just like before, in that lovely theatre, he fires another silent bullet, this time at the beloved old movie star. But the actor keeps on running, his long legs going like the clappers, waving his arms about and wailing as if he's lost his mind at the realisation of life's loveliness.

The Christmas drama Brick will play in will not end as sweetly. Angels will not get their wings but will sorely lose them. Fallen angels, falling, will fall only further. From pedestals. Will only fall downward. Into the pits.

10

A whip cracks violently across a stage floor and Ben wakes in the car, frantic with fright. David, driving still, is equally startled and jumps jittery in his seat.

"Jesus Christ! You frightened the shit out of me!"

Ben wipes the drool from the corner of his mouth and drowsily apologises.

He looks out the window to get his bearings and sees a petrol station a hundred yards down the road. His voice is panicky.

"Pull in there."

"Why?"

"I need a piss."

"I told you, should've gone before we left. It was that extra coffee you had."

David pulls in as instructed, right up alongside a vacant petrol pump, thinking he might as well get the tank filled now that they're there. He'd prefer to be done with this journey, done with driving, would prefer to be in his previous home and putting his feet up, playing something on his father's good stereo system, some classic Christmas songs booming from the speakers – that Jona Lewie one, he remembers that as a child, the bass on the singer's voice came great out of father's system, the jolly horn section ... but all in good time, all in good time.

Ben's mind has spun into overdrive. A few seconds ago he was in the middle of another dastardly dream, subjected to the torments of what he has no control over – pernicious piercings from the past – but now he is fully alert and alive in the moment, every second has become vital, from here on in nothing must go wrong, the slightest misstep and the whole thing could come tumbling down. *Jenga* was a game he played in a foster home when he was younger. A tower of wooden bricks that you built up and then ever so cautiously pulled back out one by one, placing them perilously on top of each other once again. You needed a steady hand to beat your opponent. You needed steady nerves, to make sure that the whole structure would not come falling down around you. Ben always won.

"And get some chocolate too, while I rush to the loo."

"Chocolate?" David.

"Need some sugar. Need to wake up."

"I didn't know it was allowed on your strict diet," says David shutting the door, and Ben's mind spins even further with scheme.

He sees a white van parked over at the side of the shop near the toilets. He gets out and begins bending and stretching, as if he'd been cramped and crippled by the confines of the car. He is trying to appear nonchalant, but he is eyeing up his surroundings with the focus of a preying kite. He opens the back door of the car and takes out his satchel, his head anxiously bobbing up and down, keeping an eye on the van, keeping an eye on David's activities, keeping an eye on it all. He can see David in the aisles of the shop, browsing for the right chocolate bar. A female pump attendant saunters her way breezily towards him and he's got to pretend to be a normal guy on a normal day.

"Hiya!" she says cheerily as she reaches for the nozzle and begins her operation. Ben has only time to smile a response, for he is soon sprinting away from her across the forecourt and over to the stationary white van.

The van window opens to him. Ben reaches into his satchel, takes out an envelope and slips it in. The driver in turn hands over a parcel and an envelope to Ben and he stuffs them both quickly into his satchel.

Janie Wilson, her hand on the trigger pouring petrol into David's car, is avidly watching the goings-on. Is this some kind of drug deal? Is something illicit going on? Someone stocking up for the festive season? A few little packets to really make it a white Christmas?

The man inside the van reaches over to the passenger seat – the tattoo on his neck seeming to come savagely alive as he bends, the cobra's mouth opening up even wider. He picks up a tabloid newspaper and hands that to Ben too. Ben briefly glances at the page it is folded open at – *more of it*, he thinks, *just more of it* – and he quickly shoves that into his bulky satchel along with everything else.

Ben sprints back to David's silver car, jumps into the front seat and exhales with relief.

The petrol attendant has been watching all this, trying to put a narrative on events while trying to hide her obvious suspicion. She has finished filling up the tank, replaced her petrol gun and is wondering what will happen next. Does everyone go that extra bit loopy around Christmas time? Do people lose the fucking run of themselves?

David comes out of the shop and hands Janie Wilson a ten-pound note. "Merry Christmas," he says to her and she cheerfully echoes the sentiment. Both are beaming: David proud of his good deed for the day and Janie pleased (and more than a little surprised) with the generous tip.

He gets into the car beside his boyfriend and starts the engine. He lowers the volume of the music and hands Ben over the chocolate he ordered. Ben didn't have to say which kind, David knows well enough by now: Cadbury's Bournville. Classic dark. No nuts. No fuss. Nothing gelatinous in the centre spoiling the delight of the pure chocolate bliss.

"Are you OK? You look a little out of breath there, mate. Long trip to the toilet... or more bad dreams?"

"Something like that."

"You know you need to talk to someone... anyone that went through what you wen..."

Ben, quick to ignite again, reacts with a pinched face and typical aggression:

"I didn't *go through* anything."

"What I mean is..."

Ben watches the white van pull out of the forecourt – it's just an ordinary white van going about its normal business, isn't it? Isn't that all it is?

Act normal.

Play it cool.

Draw no attention to yourself.

Still, Ben can't keep the fierceness from his voice. He feels like letting loose a tirade, putting this shit to bed once and for all:

"Look, there are always going to be orphans, parents die, or kids get abandoned, every single fucking day... not everyone is wanted. Not everyone is loved. I'm not special. I grew up...and I got over it. I'm fine. Fuck's sake. I'm perfectly fine."

It's the most he's spoken all day.

"Right, Jesus Christ, fine," says David, his face red with regret.

They still haven't pulled away from the petrol pump even though Janie has closed the cap and given the car a tap on the roof to let them know they can be on their merry way. She is standing outside the car hearing the muffled arguments and wondering what the deal is with these two guys and their mid-morning drama...and on Christmas Eve and all. They seem so ill-suited to each other, this pair. The shorter, curly one obviously affable, but the swarthy taller one seems a different beast altogether, a dark horse, no doubt about it.

Janie is just about to start walking away and leaving them to their tiff when Ben suddenly steps out of the car and stands a little too close to her for her liking.

David is open-mouthed, completely confused now, wondering if this is some kind of tactic to make him jealous – Ben has mentioned girls in the past, his first sexual experiences were with girls, David has even stored their names: Sophie, Audrey, Tracey – what the fuck is he up to here?

Ben reaches into his satchel and takes out a Christmas cracker and hands it to the girl.

"This is for you, too."

"Jeez, you two are very generous. Full of..."

"But you can't pull it yet."

"Why not?"

He smiles his best smile at her, as if making her complicit, as if to say he always plays this man of mystery role, he's good at it, and she need only put her trust in him. He is natural with girls and had plenty of practice with the girls in the orphanage. There were always kids and always around each other, clinging to each other, limbs entwined, needing, needy. They got close quickly, effortlessly, because there were no parents around, no one else to absorb their affections, no adult to reciprocate. Often they played the parts of adults themselves, experimenting with their bodies, touching each other privately, mothers and fathers, mommies and daddies, it didn't matter who was touching who, gender not really coming into play, the closeness was the thing, and it was all a way of discovering, of satisfying curiosity – as long as the nuns didn't catch you in the wicked act, there would have been Hell to pay and the beatings dished out. Slaps. Welts. Accused and then so rapidly abused. The children knew the rules, and they were all too instinctively smart and too clandestine to get caught. Wiles: most of them had them in spades. And they feared, they feared the terrible lashes. So when a small hand slid into small knickers in some closed, dank wardrobe, it would usually turn out to be some kind of success, something had been gauged, some lesson had been learned, something noted, for future usage, further adventure, which wouldn't be too far off: there were plenty of lonesome days for lonesome strays and they would always find their ways.

Ben knew all this stuff from an early age. Knew bodies inside out. He wasn't shy of girls and knew just how to handle this one here – Christmas conviviality only made the process easier.

"Sub rosa," he says.

"Sorry?"

"Secret," he says. "Keep it a secret. Just don't open it until tonight. Say about ... nine o'clock?"

She must admit she is finding herself turned on by the spontaneity of all this. It is all so unexpected. She can feel David's eyes on her in the car and she is standing there blushing, the bizarre situation of holding a Christmas cracker in her hand. What the fuck is going on? Are these gay, these two? Is she a pawn in some kind of jealousy game?

She's already gotten a tenner out of them and now a mysterious object from the tall flirty bloke too. It must be some kind of joke. It'll be a story to mull over with Patrick if nothing else. Is he not watching any of this? Where is he?

"Promise?" he pleads.

"Sure. Fine. Whatever," she says.

The "t" in *whatever* gets dropped and her *er* sounds like an *ah*, so every time she speaks she gives herself away – he knows exactly where she's from. That was another thing about his orphanage past. They came from all over the country to the Catholic-run centre, so he was able to learn to tell a West Country accent from an Essex one, a Scouse kid from a Geordie, and most of those nuns had thick Irish accents but he could still distinguish Sister Mary's Dublin brogue from Sister Bernadine's sing-song Cork lilt. It was all training. You never knew what would come in useful one day. All was training.

"Merry Christmas," he says to her, looking into her eyes so directly she feels almost violated – David in one of his more puerile moments might have even called such a move a Jedi mind-trick. He'd smash that fucking mug across…

"Same to you," she says, and turns away from Ben, cracker in hand, questions in mind.

He goes to the driver's side of the car and David lets down the window for him.

"What the hell are you up to?"

"I'm driving now. My turn. Get out."

David gets out of the car, confusion still etched on his face. Whatever weird mood Ben has been in since early morning, it is only serving to confound him even further.

Janie, from a distance, and having no other vehicle to take care of, remains agog. She won't forget these two in a hurry.

Both men buckle up their seatbelts, clacking them into their locks with undue force.

"I don't mind continuing," David says.

"I don't want to sleep," says Ben. "I want to be wide awake."

He unwraps the glossy red wrapper from the chocolate and takes a hungry snap out of it, a junkie needing his sugar rush, needing something fast, dark, immediate. He even likes this wrapper, the red and black colours appealing, perhaps arousing something primal in him. It was something he had studied, a course he had taken once: Use of Colour in Stage Design and Theatrical Props. An audience needed to see things clearly on the stage no matter where they were sitting in any given auditorium, objects shouldn't cast doubt in the mind of the audience, must be blatant; he had studied kabuki masks and their simple lines and expressions that could be viewed from any angle, viewed from distances and make complete sense. He knows the impact of actual things: toys, masks, guns. He knows the force of apparent things.

They are still parked there and Janie is still watching. It could be from a soap opera, she is sure one of them is having an affair, if not both. They can't be lovers, can they? There seems to be so much animosity between them, it practically hums.

"What was all that about?"

"You gave her a tip. So did I. Just getting into the Christmas spirit ... like you wanted."

David doubts. David worries. David has seen Ben in bed at night, shaking from whatever palsied pictures were playing out in his head.

"You sure you're all right to drive?"

"Why wouldn't I be? Anyway, you're too slow."

Ben puts his foot to the pedal, pulling away from the pumps, across the forecourt and out onto the main road with a squeak of tires and a complete disregard for oncoming traffic – luckily the coast is clear.

"Bloody hell, someone's in a hurry. Must be dying to get home for Christmas. Or else there's a bloody good party going on somewhere," says a second petrol pump attendant: Patrick Fenton has sidled up alongside his colleague watching the car disappear fast in the distance.

"That was so fucking weird," says Janie. "Two very generous guys. The driver though, one very mysterious-looking bloke. Seems like they were having a lovers' tiff at first. He gave me this."

She holds up the cracker.

Patrick raises his eyebrows, "They were gay?"

"The dark one didn't strike me as being completely gay. Maybe it was the way he looked at me."

The two attendants head away from the pumps back towards the main shop and garage area.

"Course he did," says Patrick, letting out a throaty laugh. "They all do, Janie. You're so smokin' hot."

"Fuck you."

She elbows him in the ribs and then they both stop at the shopfront, Patrick pointing upwards.

"You know the cameras got smashed in last night?"

"No, I didn't even notice."

She never notices much in the morning. She is usually late and always in a rush and flustered when she parks (badly) and clocks in. In winter she is worse; it just seems harder to get going, to get out from under the warm duvet and get her body heated and moving – too much like bloody hard work. Patrick is used to all this and is far too fond of her to give her any stick. He enjoys their camaraderie, and though she is young enough to be his daughter, she is a good sport, and he relishes what she calls *bantz*.

"I came in this morning and there was broken glass all over the ground. The two cameras done in."

"Why would someone do that?"

"Fuck knows, mate. Nothing was robbed. Too much to drink. A prank. Who knows?"

He looks around the ground to make sure there are no more pieces of broken glass, no plastic remnants.

"Fuck it, we're not going to sort it out on Christmas Eve, that's for sure. I'll call the boss on Boxing Day, he'll send someone over."

"We're not going to tell the police?"

"I'm sure they'd be none too pleased about being called out on Christmas Eve to investigate a nothing crime. Leave it till the 26th. Anyway, I wouldn't mind a drink myself. Let's get the place closed up. The year's been long enough."

Patrick starts to suddenly burst into a raucous version of "Jingle Bells", even going so far as to improvise a little dance, arms outstretched, a ballroom waltz with an invisible partner.

"Sleigh bells ring, are you listening…?"

"Fuck me, stop it right now. You'll drain whatever spirit I'm managing to cling on to."

He lets out another throaty, raspy laugh and sets off about his work, closing the lids of oil cans and throwing dirty rags into a vacant drum.

Janie looks down at the Christmas cracker she is holding in her hand, intrigued. What the fuck was all that about?

11

When Lydia Cunningham walks into the living room she finds her husband on the sofa leafing through an old photograph album.

"So the movie's finished then?"

"Just a few minutes ago. I've only seen it what, forty times now?"

"That Jimmy Stewart was always overrated. Played it too safe," she tells him. "I like the ones with edge. The brooding types. You know, the enigmatic ones."

Charles is struggling to think of an actor that fits her description, and while he wasn't a bad-looking chap himself in his day, he was certainly no matinee idol.

"For example?"

"Well, from the old days Montgomery Clift, my mother used to rave about him. Though of course we'd no idea then that he was gay. She would've been scandalised, the poor old dear. In recent times ... I don't know ... Daniel Day."

"Recent times, ha!" Charles scoffs, and the fact that she hasn't said his full name has irked him, the unwarranted familiarity of it. *Daniel Day!* Say "Lewis" for God's sake. His name was long and pretentious enough but she could still go ahead and say it right to the end.

Lydia goes to the drinks cabinet and pours herself a sherry. She's been holding out for this. It seems about the right time now; she can get away with one...or two...before her guests arrive.

Charles isn't about to let this go either.

"Not too early now, is it? Drinking time can commence then?"

"My mouth has gone all dry from saying Daniel Day's name out loud." She smirks at him. "He has that kind of effect on me."

Lydia knows how to vex him, knows the right buttons to push, the *million years* of marriage has made her quite the expert.

"Has an effect on you now, does he? That geezer must be as old as myself."

The kick of alcohol only gives her greater gumption:

"He's exactly the same age as you, as it happens. And you both such renowned actors. But you being so...different and all. In style, I mean."

She takes a calm sip of her sherry and continues before Charles has a chance to retaliate.

"He's retiring too, I hear."

"Is he? Good."

"Why *good*? Are you jealous, my sweet? That you never made it as a movie star?"

She's really got him going now. She always does this to him, this provoking, and she enjoys it. It only ever takes a sip or two. She never means it to get nasty, but she does like to poke the hibernating bear, just to hear its waking roar.

"I never wanted to be a movie star. The odd TV appearance of course. But the stage has always been more than enough for me."

"Has it now?"

She takes another sip of her drink before looking at it disappointedly – the problem with sherry glasses is that they are too bloody small, and one seems greedy if you keep going back for more.

She looks at the large photo album on Charles' lap, heavy with years of memories.

"What are you dragging that old thing out for?"

"Feeling a bit sentimental."

"That's the Jimmy Stewart effect. Works every time. Turns us all into blithering idiots. We don't shed a tear all year round and then come Christmas Jimmy Stewart picks up that child at the end and we're in floods."

"Just wanted to look back over the old Christmas ones. Look at this, David looks petrified sitting on Santa's lap."

"Wouldn't you if you were on the lap of a big hairy old man. Dodgy, those blokes."

"Just because a man wears a costume doesn't mean he's dodgy!"

Charles' face has gone red, and Lydia's not helping his blood pressure at all.

"Doesn't it? Say that to the altar boys."

"Priests don't wear costumes... oh, look, Lyd, we're not getting into all that again."

She's quite happy to let it go too. There'd been enough of all that in the media. It was sickening. And it wasn't about to end any day soon. There was always some other one hauled out over the coals, another creep done wrong to some poor kids, it was unforgivable, and it never seemed to go away.

"Are you not joining me in a drink? It is Christmas after all. We're allowed to start a little earlier. It is almost Jesus' birthday!"

"Maybe soon. I don't want to be all foolish before the boys arrive. That wouldn't look too good now, would it? Two pissed-up parents meeting the lad for the first time."

"Oh, Lord no, we have to keep up appearances."

She can be as sarcastic as she likes, but Charles feels like he's right this time, they should make a good impression, for David's sake. It is the first time he's ever brought anyone home, and they have to show him that they are supportive, encouraging, and of course they don't mind at all ... the way they are. This is a liberal family. Times have changed.

Charles takes a deep breath. She really does wind him up sometimes. That thing about priests. And Daniel bloody Day Lewis.

Lydia is staring at the Christmas tree though she seems far away. It is as if she is not looking at a tree at all but out beyond, to an audience, and she is on stage with hot lights coming down upon her. She is spot-lit ... but what on earth will she say, where are her lines?

"Doesn't it feel like we're in a play ourselves, sometimes ... acting?"

"What do you mean?"

"The two of us, our lines. The back and forth, here, in this house. But there is no one here to see us."

Charles has a dubious look about him, unsure where she is going with this.

"Maybe it's because theatre has been a part of our life, yours I mean, obviously, but mine too, vicariously. Sometimes it's like the things we say ... as if they are written for us. Like we are just characters."

She sips her sherry.

He knows what she means. He feels that way too sometimes. Even when not on the stage, when just at dinner, and one of them is saying something, and there is a silence, as if waiting for the audience to digest it. Do other families feel that way? Do other couples feel like the lights are on them? He hardly knows any other couples, hardly knows anyone anymore. People have all dwindled away. No more social functions. No one can be bothered. They say that they're too old. They stay at home. Lydia and Charles. And they watch TV. Those Nordic dramas are good, cold and distant, as if they've got nothing to do with their lives here in England; they can imagine lives elsewhere, foreign, less politically noxious, calmer perhaps, or just away, far away.

Lydia is still looking at the tree.

Charles tries to wake her out of her spell, to get them both thinking about something else. Not trees. Not drama.

"Smells good."

"What? Me or the sherry?"

"Neither. The turkey coming from the kitchen."

"The turkey is coming from the kitchen?"

Charles sighs at her silly joke, "The smell I mean. The aroma."

"I thought there for a moment I was going to get a compliment. *You smell nice Lydia darling…* new perfume? Something along that line."

"You get plenty of compliments."

"Do I?"

She puts down her drink and takes the photo album from his lap. She flicks over a page.

"Remember that tree? That artificial one? It lasted years, that mangy old thing."

"I prefer the real thing. The fresh natural smell."

Lydia laughs and points to the tree in their living room, propped there, or *trying* to stay propped there, in front of the large French windows.

"At least the old artificial one used to stand straight. We never had to worry about it falling down."

Charles cocks his head to the side. Yes, it definitely feels like the angle is all wrong, it is not quite sturdy, *precarious*, that's the word. She joins him in his study of it, both have their heads tilted now, gazing upon it, and looking past it too, beyond, out to the invisible audience who wonders what will happen next, whether this couple has lines enough to see them to the end, and wondering whether the lights will stay on in that tree, and on their stage, or whether they will be plunged into darkness.

12

Emojis coming in, pinging on David's phone. Reindeer emojis. Snowflakes. The ubiquitous Santa hats. GIFs of TV characters kissing under sprigs of mistletoe. This is the way people are saying "Merry Christmas" to each other – the younger generations hardly aware of physical cards – and there is even a message from Brendan ... so it's definitely not Ronan. Brendan. *Come back to mine.* Maybe he should have. Maybe he should have gone back to his. Too late now.

"Christmas wishes coming in thick and fast," David says mock-boastfully. "So many friends, we're so awfully popular."

Ben keeps his eyes on the road and pulls up at a traffic light. He hasn't been listening to a word David has said, something else has been on his mind.

"I'm sorry."

David looks surprised.

"For what?"

"Acting like a dick."

The light turns green and they're off again, David considering Ben's confession.

"It's OK. This has all been ... the relationship ... it's all gone a little fast ... like your driving. Slow down for fuck's sake."

Ben ignores the request and keeps going at a steady speed, below the limit, but only just.

They make their way through the festive city streets. Lights hang from overhead wires and shopfronts are preposterously decorated, alive with lights and *ho ho hos*, some garishly so.

Ben looks out at all these with typical disapproval. Some people think they can design. Some people think they can set a scene. They think they know what goes where.

"Put on the radio," he says.

"You sure?"

"They can't play Christmas songs all the time."

David sniggers, "They bloody well can."

"We might get lucky. Might get one of the good ones."

"There are good ones? Ones that you actually like?"

Ben smiles. It feels like the first time he has done this in a while.

"*I Believe in Father Christmas.*"

"I don't know that one."

"It's the best. *The Christmas you get you deserve.*"

Ben lets the line settle in the hum of the car's engine, lets David take it in before continuing:

"The singer also wishes people a hopeful Christmas and a brave New Year. Interesting word choices. Hopeful. Brave."

"A little on the dark side?"

"Maybe. But it's more honest than all the rest. It talks about seeing through people's disguises."

David looks at his partner as if seeing a side of him that rarely emerges, a man releasing thoughts and feelings instead of smothering them when they first draw breath; instead of curtness some kind of confession for a change.

"Who sings it?"

"Greg Lake."

"Never heard of him."

"You don't need to. Just that song. If you need to hear only one ... all the others pale."

David has never heard his boyfriend to be so emphatic about anything. The humdrum drive, the hum of the car, perhaps it has lulled him, hypnotised him; it seems like he has broken character, or a section of his mask has slipped – but what's underneath it? A face, sure, but that of marvel or monster?

"I'll take your word for it."

David reaches to the car radio.

"Right, here we go. Let's see if we get lucky."

They don't. When David switches it on, it is the end of a weather report and the overbearing vibes of a jolly announcer:

"... so have those heavy winter coats on if you are bracing the weather tonight – no snow, sorry to all those who were hoping for a white Christmas – but it'll be frosty for sure, with some occasional rain or sleety showers, so button up. My advice is to stay warm inside with a glass of warm punch, and on that note we'd like to remind all our listeners to drink responsibly over the holiday period and leave the car keys ..."

Ben turns the volume back down. Sure they will drink responsibly! Sure the people of England won't be on the lash for the next few days and nursing hangovers just like his boyfriend. A nation of angels. Sure they are! Sure!

David is thinking of the mysterious Greg Lake song again, "Perhaps my father will have it on CD at home. How does it go?"

"I'm not going to sing it for you!"

Ben bites the inside of his cheek, wondering how to explain the song further, it really was that rare thing – a decent Christmas pop song.

"It's about being sold a fairy story. Being lied to. And belief… or unbelief."

The words *fairy story* have ignited a memory. A young lad on a theatre stage, the painted backdrop a fairy-tale beanstalk. It must be the titular Jack that is standing there in green tights and a darker green tunic. The boy is wearing old, shabby boots – how could he climb those branches with those shabby things on his feet? But he won't be climbing anywhere. It's all just pretend. It's all just acting. There is no beanstalk. There are no magic beans either. This is a story for kids, and they can fill in most of the blanks themselves. Everybody already knows the story anyway. When the giant approaches, the kids will shout out: *He's behind you!* They know their cues, the *fee fi fo fums*. They all know them. Everybody is quite aware of what is about to occur. They know how to help Jack when he is in peril. They know the good guys and the bad. But in this flashback there are no bums on seats yet, the theatre is empty. Jack is all alone. It's eerie, the space of the place, the sense of void in an empty auditorium. You have to fill these places with words, loud words. With bodies. If it's too quiet, if there are no people watching, then it is not really a theatre at all. It's something else. Perhaps there is no name for it.

There is a loud clack as all the stage lights are suddenly turned off, the place plunged to blackness. Rehearsals must be finished for the night. The place closing up, time to go home, if you have one. But this Jack, he doesn't want the rehearsals to finish, he doesn't want to go home – doesn't really have one. He wants to keep going with it, keep playing, keep pretending that he will be the hero of the story, he wants to get to that part where he is successful, escape the clutches of the giant, get the goose that lays the golden egg and return to his mother.

A hand touches his shoulder in the darkness and the boy gasps.

Ben nearly swerves the car off the road.

"Jesus Christ," shouts David, "concentrate on what you are doing!"

"Sorry, got distracted."

"By what?"

"Doesn't matter."

They drive for a few minutes in silence, Ben hoping that song would come on the radio for David to hear. It might help him understand.

David breaks the tension by reaching out and rubbing the back of Ben's head. It's rough to the touch, recently shaved, the short bristles there, almost biting back.

"I preferred your hair long, you know."

"I know."

David is about to ask him why he would go and do such a thing, when everyone loved it the way it was. Was it Ben just being contrary? If everyone liked it why then go and chop it all off? Is that how Ben's mind works? But David notices something out the window and his attention is seized. It is a middle-aged man, clearly the worse for wear, staggering along the pavement.

"Fuck me, check out this guy. Fucking blind drunk."

The man walks straight into a lamppost and falls to the ground.

David nearly chokes with laughter.

"Shit! You wouldn't see that in a movie. I should've had my phone out. I hope he's all right. Poor fucker. Should we go back and check?"

Ben keeps his eyes on the road, the plans ahead.

"Nah. He got himself into that mess."

Bed-making. Lying in it. A cornerstone of Ben's philosophy. He has no sympathy for those that get out of their minds on booze – they deserve whatever misfortune visits them. No pity. You make your choices. He has little sympathy for alcoholics, thinking they brought it on themselves. One of the nuns let it out in a fit of rage once in the orphanage – his mother was nothing but a whore who got screwed by some foreigner and dumped the baby on them, skedaddled out of the country first chance she got, ended up walking the streets in some godforsaken shithole.

It had all come out in a torrent and the nun might have regretted her harsh and foolish tongue. But there it was. No taking it back. And the young boy had no other option but to deal with it. This is your life. This is it. You're welcome.

David removes his hand from the back of Ben's head, both of them too disappointed to touch or be touched anymore.

"After all this...when all this is over," Ben is slightly stammering, "it had nothing to do with you."

"What are you talking about?"

"It's nothing personal."

"You're starting to freak me out now...what are you..."

David's mobile suddenly rings, startling him and taking him out of a conversation he feels was about to go somewhere. He pulls it out of his jacket and sees "Mum" calling.

He tells her they are on their way.

He tells her maybe half an hour, tops.

He asks her if she is already drinking and he tries to make it light but he's not feeling that at all, feeling in no way light, there is crisp condemnation in his tone.

He pushes the phone back into his pocket, not sure where he is on the road now, not sure where he is on their journey.

Ben, eyes straight ahead, focused, reaches out and searches for David's hand. He touches it affectionately.

"It's not you."

Old chestnuts.

Roasting fires.

There is a sorrowful look about Ben.

There is a perplexed look about David.

The car though, it keeps on moving on, moving on.

13

The title of the book that sits on his lap is *Must you go? My Life with Harold Pinter* by Antonia Fraser. Charles has been meaning to read this for a while – it might even have been one of last year's Christmas presents, or the year before – but here it is now and he's only ten or eleven pages in.

As he turns the page with one hand he dips into a packet of marshmallows with the other, popping them into his mouth, chewing and half-smiling to himself. He continues to read, slowly. He's never been that good with books, with prose in general, never even bothers with a newspaper; he's better with drama, with plays printed on the page, scripts; spaces between lines always seems more convivial to him, where you can make notes, the directions clear, the words there to be spoken aloud, they make sense to him. It was something he was used to. Habits of a lifetime: hard to break.

Classical music plays on his stereo system, the one David covets and jokes about inheriting. It's Glen Gould playing Bach right now and it has the master of the house melted into a mellow mood – an easy enough state to be in when Lydia's not around to sherrily stir something up.

The mellowness doesn't last too long though, for no sooner is he enjoying her *not* being in the room than she is suddenly there, with a glower on her that tells him she is about to harass or harangue, a face he has seen many times before – what is it this time? The music too loud? Did he forget to pick up a dirty sock or put it in the wrong laundry basket? She is quite fussy about all that kind of thing, whereas Charles can happily take his foot off the pedal and go jauntily along on cruise control.

"You're not eating something, are you? Dinner will be in an hour or so!"

"Just a few marshmallows."

"Marshmallows! Where in God's name did you get those?"

"In a shop, where else?"

"But, why?"

Her confusion is reasonable: it's not every day a man in his sixties confesses so glibly to something so absurd.

"Just a whim. Just saw them … they're bloody glorious."

"You'll spoil your appetite."

"Not at all. These things are so light; they're not in the least bit filling. In fact, they practically disappear the moment you put them in your mouth."

He does exactly that now, right in front of her, puts a marshmallow in his mouth and delights in its disappearance. If only all the actions of the world could be so simple and reliable.

"They're so insignificant," he says. He could mean the whole human enterprise. He could mean man's place in a hostile and ever-expanding universe. But he doesn't, he's more literal-minded than that. He just means marshmallows.

Charles closes the book and places it on the sofa. He cannot concentrate now. Not if she keeps butting in on him like this.

Lydia goes and pours herself another sherry from the drinks cabinet. He looks at her, amazed that she always seems to have a glass on her person, as if she has the ability to magically conjure one at will, some slick sleight of hand trick gleaned on a housing estate in Glasgow – does she just keep them in her pockets, up her sleeves?

"I got a mad craving when I saw them there in the supermarket last week. I felt I just had to have them. Looked irresistible. Odd craving, eh? Out of nowhere. I just couldn't stop myself."

He holds up the packet in front of his own face, inspecting it, scanning the ingredients to see what each one contains. Where do they even come from? Who makes such tender beauties? Imagine the smells in a place like that, a marshmallow factory, imagine what goes on there. Conveyor belts of them passing by, each more succulent than the last, more than you'd ever know what to do with. The notion is intoxicating.

"They remind me of my childhood. The taste. The texture. Brings it all back. The good old days... when we were young and vital."

Lydia rolls her eyes, "Is that from some play you were in?"

"No, but maybe I should write one. A play about just that. My younger, wilder days. Days of secret savagery. I'll call it *Marshmallows*. Not a bad idea, actually."

He eats another with a sort of gleeful gluttony and then sticks out the packet to offer her one, a peace offering, if she will, an offer to join him in what is either childishness or licentiousness, hard to decide which, but she shakes her head in a robust refusal.

"It's one of these you should be having," she tells him, holding up her own glass. "Or something stronger. Marshmallows, for fuck's sake. Regressing, is that what you're doing? Retreating to your formative years? Marshmallows, at your age!"

They both feel the absurdity of their peccadilloes, her sherry, his sweets, and both are stubborn enough not to let go.

"They're perfect for people of our age. The nearly toothless! The gummy old folk of the world! You don't even need teeth for these. They're so soft and easy. Not like a toffee which will fight you all day long. You'd be scraping the stuff out of your fillings forever."

He smiles at the thrust of his own argument; surely the case can be put to rest.

"At least you haven't opened the box of Quality Street yet."

"There's a box of Quality Street?"

"I've hidden them."

"Maybe that's for the best."

"Put those bloody things away now, you'll have no mind for the turkey."

Charles hands over the packet of marshmallows to his wife like a naughty child, the case then is finally closed, and he feels he's the one been unjustly convicted.

"And you can turn off that maudlin music and all. Don't want the boys coming into a house that sounds like a funeral parlour. Put something Christmassy on."

"I don't think we have anything *Christmassy*, although... there was that Michael Bublé one floating around last year. Where's that gone?"

Lydia tops up her sherry a little more, under his watchful and not a little condescending eye. She ignores his intimations of contempt. She has no idea where that Bublé album has gone, or where the years have gone, she has no idea what will happen to the two of them if they are to be together all day in this big house – the trip to Greece is to be part meditation on just such a notion. The future.

"I called David," she says, this another magician's misdirecting manoeuvre to distract him from her drinking. "They'll be here in twenty minutes or so."

"Right. Right," he says, as if he'd almost forgotten the occasion.

"You can go back to reading your book."

He frowns.

"What book?"

"That one there beside you. The one I got you for Christmas last year and you still haven't read."

Charles picks up the book and looks at it, bewildered. Had he even started this book? It does look awfully familiar. The cover of it. The weight. The book is purportedly about playwright and poet Harold Pinter, author of *The Birthday Party* and *The Caretaker* among others. Those menacing plays, funny and frightening in equal measure. Harold. Fine gentleman. Not afraid to get political. Tough as old boots. Has Charles started reading this book about the great man? He was so involved in eating those dainty marshmallows... they were so soft and easy. So light. They were no trouble at all. Would it were that everything were so easy to consume, and without consequence.

"I met him once," he says to his wife, "Pinter. Harold Pinter. He wrote that one... recently... I played a part in it, and..."

Lydia takes a swig of her drink and tops up her glass again with a devil-may-care tilt of the bottle, filling it as far as it will go without spilling over onto her hand. It could be a long day, this day, it could be very long, and these sherry glasses are much too small. He doesn't even remember, has no clue where that book even came from, how it even came to be in the house. And she's pretty sure he never met Harold Pinter in his life. He would surely have mentioned it in one of his dreary anecdotes at some dreary après-party. No wonder she drinks.

Charles is now looking at the Christmas tree. The lights are flashing, on, off, on and off. The rhythm never changes, it stays constant, never given to whimsy, never capitulating to caprice; he's not sure if this is comforting or terrifying; one could champion either corner. He wonders how long those lights could go on without a bulb breaking, without giving up one of their tiny ghosts. Would they go on forever, or does everything eventually burn out? He has none of these answers, but he stares at the tree anyway, knowing what a bad fist he's made of it.

14

Supermarkets become fewer, pound shops disappear, retail establishments of any description generally dwindle and roads darken as the car wends its way from city streets into what might be termed *countryside*. There are fields in evidence now, full hedges, tall trees, and the flickering fairy lights are restricted to the windows of large, respectable homes – effort has clearly been put into these to be tasteful: gentle golds, classy silvers, not gaudy pinks.

This is Charles Cunningham's neighbourhood, a far cry from the tight dwelling place of his son, far from pokey flats piled up on wedged-in buildings crammed up against one another – apartments, the word more respectable, more buoyant than "flat". This here is all about green, foliage and fullness, a place of space, a place of quiet, of obvious affluence, a place to aspire to, or a place for those who got dealt a good hand, fell on their feet, got lucky with the breaks.

Ben pulls the car right up to the big black railings of the Cunningham property – he might even be tempted to call it Charles' *estate*, but he is unsure of the nomenclature, all he knows is that it is wide and enviable and those gates were designed to keep the likes of him and his mates strictly on the outside, unless they came to mend something, cut the sweeping lawn.

David gets out of the car and goes to the chrome panel mounted on the side pillar. Needs to key in the security code.

It becomes time for Ben to get busy. Quickly he takes his phone out of his pocket and dials a number. The other side responds with an ursine grunt.

"Wait," says Ben, and he rests the phone at the side of his right leg, making sure it is neatly concealed.

When David keys in the four-digit code, the gates of Eden begin to slide open. For comic effect he does a theatrical Moses-like gesture as if he is parting the waves – this is all for Ben's amusement, though Ben couldn't care less and is more interested in getting on with what's really at stake.

David sits back in the passenger seat and Ben starts moving the car slowly into the grounds, the tyres crunching on the hard gravel.

"Great that you can remember the code," he says to David, loud enough for his phone to pick it up. "Even in your hungover state."

"I don't think 1957 is a very difficult one to remember," says David, laughing.

"1957?" Ben repeats. "Significant?"

"Only the year of his birth. Could it be any fucking simpler?" David shakes his head at the idiocy of it. "Although it's probably best that it's kept that simple, I'm not sure his memory is what it used to be."

They proceed down the long driveway at a crawling pace at David's request. He wants Ben to take in the impressive surroundings, a feeling of excited pride tingling the hairs at the back on his neck. The place is splendid, it really is, and to think it will all be his someday: David, the Cunninghams' only heir.

"I don't know how the fuck he remembers his lines on stage. That last one, *No Man's Land*, ironically, is all about memory, or the loss of it."

Ben is nodding, pretending to give a shit. The phone stays live by his side – he cannot quit that call just yet.

"Does he have any other security, I mean … is that it? I'd imagine there are lots of valuables in the house, he needs to be careful."

"Nah, that's it. He had a dog once. A long-legged Doberman. It died though. Old age. Othello. Typical, eh? For a big bastard of a dog it was actually pretty tame. Kind of a disappointment. It's pretty safe around here. A good Neighbourhood Watch community, and the cops come out and check up on things sometimes. Not over the Christmas season though, I suppose."

Ben surreptitiously turns off the phone at his side. Another job done.

They pull up in front of the house.

"All righty then," says David, then taking a deep breath. He sputters, "Shit, it's me who's nervous now."

"Don't worry. It'll all be fine."

"Just try not to be your usual grumpy self. Act nicely."

"Act! Of course. We've come to the right place for that."

"Seriously," says David, surprised at the way his own body is suddenly a-quiver. "Eyes and smiles, my sweet. Eyes and smiles. Show off your best attributes."

David doesn't catch Ben mutteringly repeat this phrase, nor does he see Ben hawking up a glob of phlegm and gobbing it right there on the gravel, an animal marking his new territory.

In a white van, parked and idling, Brick Herbert keys in the number 1957 on his smartphone. He waits. A few spatters of rain fall on the windscreen and he watches the drops make their tracks down. He is a patient man. When you've spent time on the inside you learn to become patient, to appreciate little things on the outside. 1957. Fucking hell. That was easy.

In a cramped flat, with cardboard boxes littering the living space, his twin does push-ups on the floor. Loud, thumping EDM plays and he moves to the rhythm of it, his massive muscles visible under the tight T-shirt; sweat glistens, veins bulge; the eyes of the cobra on the side of his neck are a striking red.

Despite the loud music he hears his phone ping on the nearby coffee table. He picks it up and sees the message from his brother. *1957*, followed by the words: *We're on.*

He smiles to himself and flings the phone onto an armchair and resumes his exercising – he ramps up the tempo as the music dictates. On the inside you learned to keep in shape; you needed your strength, all of it, and your senses became hyperaware. 1957. Fucking hell, he thinks. That was easy.

The grand door of the grand house opens and Lydia is there and it is she who is all eyes and practised smiles.

The man of the house appears behind her equally tall and imposing, both used to being seen and knowing how to make an impression. Charles stands proudly, chest inflated, as if a director has called him in for an audition and he is putting his best foot forward.

"Come in, come in," he says with a voice so sonorous he could be trying out for the role of Dracula. Ben wonders if it is an affectation, or whether he always sounds like this when he's off stage, when the camera is not trained on him.

"It's great to finally get to meet you," Charles says sticking out his hand, which Ben takes and firmly shakes.

"Likewise. I've heard so much. And of course I've followed your career with interest."

"Nice of you to say so. I hear you're in the theatre business yourself."

"Nothing special. Just the props guy. Occasional set design."

"A very important guy! Come on in; no point in us all standing here in the doorway. Go into the living room there and get yourselves nice and warm."

David receives a great hug from his mother and goes about lugging in the bags from the car – his boyfriend leaves him at it, offering no assistance.

Ben scans the living room, trying as quickly as he can to get his bearings. He could be a ten-year-old again, brought to a new home and trying to acclimatise as quickly as possible, to know where everything is, to know how best to get out if he needs to escape.

"David, dear," says Lydia, "why don't you take those bags upstairs out of the way? Then we'll all have a little drink before dinner."

"Naturally," he responds, trying not to sound snide.

Ben reaches out and snatches his own satchel from him – he'll be needing that. The crackers. His stuff. He'll be needing all his stuff.

David, dogsbody now and sighing about it, moves out of the room and begins heaving the luggage up the stairs, banging both himself and the bags off the walls as he sways his way upwards.

In the living room Ben is invited to sit down and is asked what he'll have.

"Oh, not fussy, whatever's going."

"My darling wife has already started before us."

Lydia frowns, she's never sure whether he is out to embarrass her or to make himself out to be superior – if Ben could only have seen him earlier with his little bag of sweeties.

"But I think I'll have a glass of wine," Charles says, "I got a lovely bottle of red from a friend of mine, was saving it for a special occasion."

Lydia is trying to think who that friend might be. There aren't too many left. He probably just bought it himself, along with his marshmallows. What a lonely figure he must've cut in that supermarket.

"And this has to be one, am I right? A special occasion?"

Ben cannot agree more, "It certainly is."

Charles takes the bottle from the drinks cabinet and looks around for a corkscrew.

"I could've sworn there was one here."

"There is," says Lydia, "over to your left."

Charles finds it and stands squinting at the label on the bottle, suggesting his "friend" does indeed have exquisite taste.

"Old age, son, the eyes aren't what they used to be."

Ben winces at the word 'son'. He was never anyone's son, no matter what foster home he found himself staying in. How dare he toss around a word so carelessly.

But Ben can smother this embryonic ire.

Ben knows better.

Ben can smile it off.

"The ears are going too. Lucky the memory is still intact. Sharp as a tack. Auditions for Lear coming up soon. Think it might be my last hurrah."

Lydia is shaking her head hoping their guest will take notice. He does.

"I think you'd be superb in that role," fawns Ben, knowing he'll have to do a lot of acting himself this evening.

"Oh, well, we'll see," says Charles, "one of the trickier roles, isn't it? You didn't see my Prospero by any chance did you?"

Lydia is looking at him holding the bottle in one hand and the corkscrew in the other. Is he going to open the fucking thing or just stand there pontificating?

"No, I'm afraid not," says Ben. "I don't get to see many plays, even though I design stuff for them occasionally. It's mostly movies I do these days. I'm involved in a company that makes masks, replica items, stuff like that. Just...fake stuff. I design a lot on computer."

"Yes, yes, of course, that's the way it is these days. I could've gone down the movie route myself, but I never had much interest. Prefer to tread the boards, the opening night nerves, the breaking of legs...you know how it is."

Lydia has to force herself to not roll her eyes and she does her best to stifle an already-bored yawn. She is still looking at the unopened bottle and will grab it herself if he doesn't get a move on.

"Of course," says Ben, "a big performance. I get it. Nothing like it. Very exciting."

Charles finally has a go at removing the cork from the bottle, but it is proving to be more difficult than he had thought.

Lydia grabs the bottle and corkscrew from him, but despite her huffing efforts she finds herself struggling too.

It is time for new boy Ben to make his first mark. Such a pity David is not here to see this – what is taking him so long upstairs? Is he rifling through drawers searching for loose change? Or is he trying to locate those all-important business papers which will say for sure that everything, the entire estate, will be left to him?

Ben pulls out the cork in one clean pop.

"Great to have a strong man around the place," says Charles. "You keep fit by the look of you."

They hold out their glasses and Ben pours each of them a glassful. He is careful with his serving and careful to allow himself only a half. Got to keep his wits about him.

"What's the word they use now?" says Lydia, "I heard it on the TV the other day. *Gym rat*, isn't that the term? Sounds awfully American. And awfully vulgar."

"I know," says Ben. "Horrible phrase. But yeah, I suppose I am. I work out two or three times a week. I've tried to get David to come but he won't budge."

The timing couldn't be more perfect as the subject of the conversation enters the room.

"Talking 'bout me behind my back then?"

"Just saying how I tried to get you to join the gym with me."

"Oh, here we go. Next it'll be complaints about going out and…"

Lydia takes on the role of peacemaker, the house has had quite enough tension already. She raises her glass, the first toast of their day, and addresses them sternly:

"Listen you two, you are both young and have your whole lives ahead of you. Enjoy yourselves while you can. Make the most of it."

They raise their glasses and David has to go to the cabinet and pour his own to join in their little ceremony.

And Lydia isn't finished yet. She has already been quite lubricated by her morning libations, her tongue is loose and her lines lilting:

"Whatever it is that keeps you motivated. Make the most of it."

She points at her husband and smirks.

"You'll be as old as him before you know it."

"Oi, cheeky," says Charles, pretending to be unruffled but clearly stung. "There's life in this old dog yet. I was just telling Ben here that rehearsals for *The Tempest* are coming up soon."

Ben and Lydia look at each other.

"*The Tempest*, love? Are you sure?"

"Rehearsals in January. I'm quite looking forward to it."

"*The Tempest?*" says Lydia again, pressing him to remember.

It has been like this of late, little things, slips of the tongue, misplaced items, anecdotes he can't recall (previously recounted effortlessly with a raconteur's wit and unbecoming pomp). He looks simply confused now. He takes a sip of his wine as if that might jog something.

"*King Lear*," prompts Ben, generously.

"Yes," says Charles. "What did I say?"

"*The Tempest*," says Lydia.

"No, no. I did that one before ... *King Lear*. Yes. Yes. Lear."

He pauses, takes another sip of his wine and then in the same Christopher Lee voice with which he welcomed Ben at the door, unleashes a few lines of Shakespeare's masterpiece, to let them know that he has indeed still got what it takes:

"*Thou but rememberest me of mine own conception. I have perceived a most faint neglect of late, which I have rather blamed as mine own jealous curiosity than as a very pretence and purpose of unkindness. I will look further into't. But where's my fool? I have not seen him this two days.*"

Ben starts clapping vociferously, smiling widely, "Wowza."

Lydia can only stoop to sarcasm, "Remarkable. He can recite lines of Shakespeare at length but can never remember to put the bins out."

They laugh at her jibe, but Lydia prays that will be the end of it; enough with the showing off. She wants a normal day for a normal *new* family.

She tells them that she will check on the bird in the oven, and she leaves them at it, carrying her drink with her, for the journey to the kitchen.

David stands near the fireplace. The nervousness hasn't yet abated and he looks from face to face trying to gauge their impressions. Are they getting on well, these two? Do they actually like each other? They do have something in common: the theatre (although one of them is far less pretentious about it). Is Father going to continue reciting lines and boring the pants off everyone for the entire afternoon? Is Mother going to drink too much and make a complete arse of herself – it wouldn't be the first time.

Ben looks pleased though, at least that. The early morning petulance seems to have vanished and a geniality taken over. Perhaps he is just an actor too. Perhaps everyone has their part to play.

Ben notices the book on the sofa. He puts his glass on the coffee table and picks it up.

"Any good?" he says, gently leafing through it.

Charles looks at it curiously, "I don't know. I haven't started it yet."

"I like Pinter's stuff. *The Birthday Party* was a huge influence on me. The way the banal grew so menacing, and so quickly. One minute you think you are in an ordinary boarding house and the next ... well ... terrifying."

David is nodding, impressed.

Ben continues:

"It's by his wife, isn't it? That book. They say they had a very strong relationship."

"Maybe so," says Charles. "I'll have to find time to read it. Very busy you know."

"Did you ever meet him?" asks Ben. "Pinter. When he was alive."

"No, I don't think so. Can't say that I have."

David is once again eyeing up that stereo system and can't help breaking in on their conversation.

"Great speakers on this."

"Should be. It bloody well cost enough. Was playing some lovely classical music earlier but your mother made me turn it off; said I was being maudlin."

"Well, not sure if we can play any Christmas music either, Ben gets all grumpy."

"That's not true," says Ben, "I love Christmas music! Even the carols, you know the old-fashioned ones."

Ben is smiling at Charles benignly, knowing that David is watching and disapproving of his barefaced lies.

"I love the traditional stuff, too," Charles says cheerily. "David, have a root around there, see if you can find anything. Lyd was looking for one earlier, Sinatra or something. Couldn't find it."

David searches cabinets and rummages around in drawers and eventually stumbles upon *A Very Special Christmas*.

"Not exactly traditional," he says, "but it'll have to do."

"Great!" says Ben with such ersatz enthusiasm that David has to choke back his laugh.

The Pointer Sisters kick off the album with "Santa Claus Is Coming to Town" and the three men hold their wine glasses and stand awkwardly in the large living room, each trying to think of something to say.

Ben looks at the elegant Christmas tree, but before he can present a compliment he cocks his head ever so slightly, wondering if the thing is not slightly tilting.

"I know, I thought the same thing," says Charles. "Lopsided, isn't it?"

"No, it's fine, really. It's charming."

"*Charming?*" says David. "Well, we've got all the appropriate words today. Seriously Dad, this is a very different person from the one we had in our kitchen this morning."

"I wasn't the one that was hungover," spits Ben.

"Rough night was it, son?"

"Just enjoying the festive season, that's what it is there for isn't it?"

"I suppose so. You'll be back to college in a few weeks … and you'd better make some headway with that thesis of yours."

"Don't remind me, I..."

They have no chance to rally back and forth about David's studies, the lack of commitment he displays, about how he cannot afford to waste any more time, because Lydia is bellowing from the dining room, ordering them to come and get it.

"Gentlemen, start your engines," says David, who realizes that he is seriously hungry. He hasn't eaten anything all day – couldn't stomach the idea of it this morning after the revels of the night before. But the smells are seducing him now, and he thinks he just might be able to cope with a few mouthfuls of that turkey meat drowned in cranberry sauce, it might make him human again.

Charles leads the way and the younger men follow, David childishly giving Ben a thumbs-up behind Charles' back to let him know that he is performing exceptionally well.

Ben looks at the walls as he follows the master of the house, taking in the photos and the paintings and framed theatre posters that adorn the walls.

"Sorry, Mr. Cunningham, this one here, is it famous?"

Charles turns around, the wine almost swirling out of his glass.

"You've a good eye there. Yes, a Lucian Freud sketch. Original. A gift for my fiftieth birthday from Lydia. Worth a few bob now I should think. And it's *Charles*, please. No *misters* around here. No need for formalities here, son."

Ben flashes a false smile through gritted teeth – inside he seethes sorely.

He was never anybody's son. Never was. Never will be.

All three enter the dining room where a knife is being sharpened for carving.

15

White Van Man. Yes, it's a cliché now, a meme maybe, but so what, he is what he is; he drives a white van.

He's driving it now, on Christmas Eve, working, always working, always on the job. It's the way he likes it. His brother, on route as well, exactly the same. Not only do they have the same facial features, but their desires, their habits, their hobbies and interests, they hardly vary. And they work together. In tandem. It's a lot faster with two on the job.

Their differences are few: the cobras on their necks are at different sides and they glow with differently coloured eyes, and today Brick wears a black bomber jacket, while Brac's – though identical in size, shape and material – is an ox-blood red.

Band Aid's "Do They Know It's Christmas?" is playing on the radio and Brick remembers being at a pub quiz once when the question master asked the teams to name at least five of the singers that performed on that song. Brick had been drinking a pint of bitter at the bar and not taking part in the quiz but in his mind he was going through them, even though the song was a little bit before his time: Boy George, George Michael, Bono. Brick really doesn't take too much notice of what happens in the pop charts, if they even have charts anymore. He does like music, especially when it's full of rhythm, when it thumps hard, when it gets the blood up, especially when exercising, when he's pumping weights. He likes those Sleaford Mods. At last you had a pair who was telling you the truth about the way things are in the country. Not lying to your face. Not trying to put one over on you. They give it to you straight. They don't mince their words. No nonces, those boys. No nonsense. Nottingham lads, but fuck it, no one's perfect. What song told it straighter than "Jobseeker" or "Fizzy"? Solid blokes. Knew a good tune and kept it simple. No faffing about.

The bells are ringing on this song now and they are all making impassioned pleas for the starving who live in a place where no rain or rivers flow. Fuck this shit. Fuck it. Brick turns it off.

In an identical van and with an identical pout Brac Herbert harrumphs and turns the radio off as well. Fuck that bullshit and all the other Christmas songs can go and fuck right off and all. He is sick to death of them now. He even found himself whistling them at odd moments despite himself – they just crept into your head and lodged there. Like parasites. Feeding off you. Sapping your energy. Sapping your right-mindedness. When he stops at a traffic light he pulls out a Sleaford Mods CD from the glove compartment and slips it in the player. That's better. Those geezers know what they are doing. Telling it like it is.

The twins have a job to do. The twins always have a job to do. They are always on the go. Always keeping busy. White van men.

They keep themselves in shape.

They keep good time.

They keep to themselves.

There are only a few people they work with, only a few they can bring themselves to trust.

They keep it simple.

They are working tonight.

Do they know it's Christmas?

Yeah, fucking right they do, but that doesn't stop them from getting out and doing a bit of work, getting the job done, there's always money to be made. Always trade.

Jason Williamson of Sleaford Mods is spitting out his lyrics, saying that some of the smelly bastards need executing. James Williamson would probably have no trouble executing some of the perverts you read about in the rags every day. He would not take any shit from them.

The twins are bobbing their heads. Fuck yeah. It is good to be alive and on the job, doesn't matter the season, the occasion. Work is work, a deal is a deal and they know a decent tune when they hear one.

So, driving, on the job.

Getting things done.

Out to clean up the shit, exterminate the vermin.

White van man times two.

White vim men.

ACT II

16

A single, emaciated tree on a bare stage. It's the kind of tree that would not hold you were you to try and hang yourself, its branches too twiggily timid.

The director, a man as tall and gaunt as the tree he observes, looks worried. Is the set design bold enough? Stark enough to match the themes of the play? He's worried about the actors too, the rehearsals have not been going as smoothly as he'd expected. Lack of concentration? No, it isn't that. Something more elemental. Fire. That's what's lacking. There is no fire in their bellies. Hardly a spark. And the show just weeks away from opening.

He adjusts his long white ponytail and steps further back on the stage – something is still not quite right, perhaps the tree needs to be pushed a little more to the centre. A few inches down their country road. Maybe.

A cry from the boy backstage draws him away from his concerns. He drops all the notes he has been carrying and rushes towards the wings.

A boy runs past him, sobbing. And it's not just any boy, it's *THE* boy, the one who will stand on this very stage and tell the two tramps that Mr. Godot would not be coming. It's that boy. The boy under his tutelage, at least for the duration of the production.

The boy is too fast and the director lets him run off down through the theatre. As he runs he drops something, a sweet packet. The director picks it up: an empty packet of marshmallows. He'll have to talk to the boy later, find out exactly what happened. The advice was always to never work with children, they were too unpredictable, but he had no choice, the play required one.

The man playing the character of Pozzo suddenly appears on the stage. He is in his dress-rehearsal garb: pot-bellied, moustachioed, and bulging with the haughtiness of the slave master he has been practising all day. His belt buckle hangs open and he carries a whip which he drops noisily to the floor. He tidies up his trousers, tightening his belt. He is chewing on something.

"It's Estragon's trousers that are supposed to fall down, not mine," he jokes, to the startled director.

"The boy ... is he all right?"

"Oh, him, yes, he's fine. Children eh, always moaning about something or other. And I bought him some sweets and all. Soft things they are. And quite addictive."

The director looks at him. The director doubts.

"This whip," huffs the actor. "It doesn't crack."

"Crack?"

"When I use it. When I try to whip the floor in front of Lucky, it doesn't make a bloody sound. It's not loud enough, I mean. A proper cracking sound. It's too light. Can't you get a better one?"

"Um, yes, I suppose so," the director's Adam's apple clearly bobbing in his thin neck, "I'll see what I can do. I think though, you should be focusing more on ... we open in just ..."

The actor leaves the director with a flawless imitation of his squeaky voice: *I'll see what I can do*. He climbs down from the stage and walks down through the centre aisle, in the direction of the vanished boy. He casts the ineffectual whip aside, not particularly caring where it lands.

17

"Ta-daaa!"

Lydia places the succulent roast turkey on the table in front of them. It sits there steaming and fat, surrounded by a ring of mini Yorkshire puddings.

Surrounded by some hungry humans too.

"My word, darling, but you've certainly outdone yourself this time."

Many of David's friends have become vegans, and he has poked fun at their bleeding-heart liberalism, their woke-ishness, their waifish-ness, but he's glad he's not eschewed meat, not on a day like today: his mouth madly moistens at the sight and the smell.

"Looks amazing, Mrs. Cunningham," says Ben, impressed by the middle-class spread, something he has never really seen before. Many of the care homes he was sent to were middle class all right, or at least aspired to be, but the wealth and comfort was very much on show here, nothing but the finest ware, cutlery, delectables; no doubt as to what kind of house you were in – he feels extremely out of place.

Charles wags a finger at him, "What did I say about formalities?"

"He's right, Ben. It's Lydia," says his wife, hoping that the matter is finally resolved.

"Ben says he has never had Brussels sprouts before. Can you believe that?" says David.

"This should be quite the experience then. Go on, try one," urges Charles.

Ben, slightly embarrassed, boldly sticks out his fork and impales one of the round, green, leafy balls. It doesn't taste all that bad... though not great either. He nods his approval all the same. Why does David have to go and make a big fuss about it? Is it about putting people in their place? Knowing where you are?

"Is it Brussel's sprouts or Brussel sprouts? Is there an apostrophe, I mean?" asks David.

"God, I'm not even sure," says his father. "Never thought about it. Don't get too excited Ben, they're the least impressive things on the table."

"Charles, will you do the honours, darling?"

The master of the house rises at his wife's request and receives the large carving knife as if on ceremony.

"Mind what you are doing," she tells him. "We don't want any injuries before we go travelling."

"Travelling?"

"Tomorrow."

Charles looks at her, a shadow of confusion clouding him once again.

"To Greece. Tomorrow," she says.

"Yes, yes, of course. Don't look at me like I've forgotten. I haven't you know. I'm not senile yet."

David and Lydia exchange a look. Sixty-two is not old these days. The media would have you believe you are nothing but a whippersnapper. But they are also aware that Charles' father had Alzheimer's, and Charles' memory has been evading him of late. Nothing to worry about he tells them, they were overreacting.

"Here goes," he says, making a theatrical swipe with the blade through the air. Calmly he brings the serrated edge of it onto the flesh of the turkey and expertly cuts and slices. Lydia helps him apportion equally onto everyone's plate.

When everyone is seated and ready to tuck in, Lydia raises her glass. Another toast.

"Merry Christmas everybody!"

Ben admires the cut of the glass as he drinks. Nothing spared. Not on this day. Not a thing wrong with the food either, Lydia no slouch in the kitchen – the drinking doesn't seem to hamper her skills one bit.

"Well, I must say it's lovely having you home, David," says his father, "and the first time you've brought a … are we allowed say *boyfriend*? You know with all the terminology these days we have to be careful what we say."

David looks at his father thinking it would be far better if he said nothing at all.

"*Boyfriend* is fine," says Ben. "We're not fussy about what people say."

It had been playing on Charles' mind. People take offence these days so easily. Everybody irate about something or other. In the theatre there are people of all colours, all creeds, all … propensities. They all have secrets. What happened in the past should stay there. Everyone made mistakes.

"We've become a great society in that we can have such relationships," Lydia chips in.

"Indeed," agrees her husband, "in our days things were quite different. You'd be... punished."

David shakes his head in mild embarrassment. This was bound to happen. Different generations coming together like this and trying to make sense of a new world where new things happen at astonishing speed, bound to cause friction. He remembers when he first told his mother and father, when he first came out. They had taken the whole thing remarkably well. Had they always known? Most probably. The posters on his bedroom wall were a dead giveaway – not one female pop star ever got put up. His mother and father hugged him then and sent him off to college and told him he could be whoever he wanted to be, just to be careful, and to not get himself in trouble. Trouble is something that *lingers*, his father had said, and might never go away. *Be good and be careful and don't hurt*, those were his exact words. Does his father remember that advice from all those years ago? Or has all that slipped by too? They are getting old. They are all getting old. David will get serious. He made resolutions already today, in the shower as the water cascaded down upon him, as his boyfriend made innocent Christmas crackers at the kitchen table, he told himself that he'd have to get things right. A new year was about to be thrust upon them. Best to seize it, and make it right.

"Why don't you tell us some stories about your days in the theatre, Mr... Charles."

"Oh, for God's sake, don't encourage him," says David, sounding like his mother and more exasperated than he had intended.

"I don't mind at all," says Charles, warming to his son's boyfriend even more, his cheeks flushing from the wine and the sense of the day's success. He puts down his knife and fork, intertwines his fingers, and lets his hands rest on his belly. He sits back in his chair and lets his long legs stretch out under the table.

"Lots of great days over the years. Not all rosy of course. The pauper years, the bad reviews, par for the course. There weren't too many of those, thankfully. One critic once said – in *The Times Literary Supplement*, no less – *one of the finest actors ever to grace the boards of London, or any stage anywhere*. Now, that was some compliment back then I can tell you. And I was only, what, in my late thirties I suppose."

He catches Lydia's glare. She wants him to stop. But he is only getting warmed up. Warming to his subject. To this occasion. Warm. Yes, it all feels very warm. He can easily sidestep whatever glare she throws at him.

"I've got the cut-out somewhere. A scrapbook I've kept over the years. Not that I'm being put out to pasture just yet, Ben, you understand. There's to be a production of Lear, next year, they're casting for it in a few weeks. I wouldn't be surprised at all if my agent gives me a call. She's a funny one, Dorothy. My old agent died you see, Trevor Evenson. Fine gent. Fine gentleman indeed. The best you could hope for. Heart attack. Wouldn't you know? He was too bloody fond of those cigars if you ask me. Good thing no one smokes those bloody things anymore. Disgusting. Disgusting things. His poor wife found him on the bedroom floor one afternoon. Just lying there. Poor old Trev. A great man to cut a deal. Took no prisoners. Got me ... well, got me where I am today. But it's Dorothy that takes care of my bookings now. *Door Open Dot.* That's what I call her. It's one of her stock phrases, always talking about *doors opening.* A rather bland metaphor for opportunity but still, bless her, she works hard for me. I'm sure she'll make the Lear thing happen."

A thought suddenly assaults him and his face falls.

"But we won't be here, Lyd! We'll be in Spain!"

There is a prickly petulance to his outburst, as if his wife is all to blame.

"It's Greece, love. And there's no need to panic, we'll be back here in plenty time. We're only going for eight days."

Lydia takes a gulp of wine, Dutch courage for her next gambit.

"And I don't think you should be going for any new parts anyway. Time you relaxed, don't you think? You've done more than enough. Leave it to the young men and women. The next generation. It's their turn."

Charles takes a forkful of meat to his mouth and chews almost violently. He takes a serious swig of wine to wash it all down and gets boldly to his feet.

"Lear needs an older gentleman as you all well know. A young Lear would be preposterous! You wouldn't have an old Hamlet, now, would you? Wouldn't make any bloody sense!"

He looks around the table at the three who have stopped eating and are surprised by his overreaction.

"I still have it you know. Talent! Talent! It's still there," he beats his chest, right there where his hidden heart lies.

Ben is doing his utmost to conceal a smirk; he had not been expecting this little drama to take place – his drama is to happen later, with him as the director, this is all very surprising, a moment of unexpected, unadulterated fun.

Charles clears his throat and pompously prepares. He takes another swig of wine and clears his throat again.

"When we are born we cry that we are come to this great stage of fools. This is a good block: It were a delicate stratagem to shoe a troop of horse with felt."

He allows himself to get even more animated, delighted with this moment he has brazenly attained: an audience of three staring up at him.

"I'll put it in proof and when I have stolen upon these sons-in-law, then, kill, kill, kill, kill, kill, kill!"

Well, what on earth can they say to that?

Absolutely nothing.

They have even stopped chewing.

All three of them, they can do nothing but gawp.

"Jesus Christ," says Lydia eventually, "there's a lovely speech for the Christmas dinner table. *Kill kill kill!"*

David and Ben join her in a timid, good-natured laughter while Charles looks suddenly deflated and slumps back down onto his chair.

He looks at Ben. Has he seen this lad before? His face looks awfully familiar. He must surely have run into him in some theatre before. Rehearsals at some point? Putting the final touches to some set, something like that, the lad handing him a prop just before he trod out under the hot lights; Ben would have mentioned something surely... but this face, this face before him...

Lydia lifts up the empty wine bottle and decides to go and get another, but before she even has a chance to rise Ben has already anticipated her movements and is quick to assist.

"Please. Allow me. I brought a bottle. It's in my bag in the living room."

"You're just full of surprises," says his cynical boyfriend, something else David didn't know about. He is always impressed by Ben's athleticism, the way he can just spring up out of a chair like that, almost simian in strength and agility; the gym, he supposes, that bloody gym: it has made Ben lithe and David loathe – David can hardly ever get up out of a chair without feeling dizzy.

Christmas, thinks Ben as he leaves the dining room, *a time for giving and receiving*. It is in every bad song and every bullshit greeting card and it echoes something said to him many years ago, behind a pantomime beanstalk. Dark shadows there. Lights off after a show. A boy in his green tights, green tunic, shabby boots. *A time for giving and receiving.* The giant had chuckled at what he must have thought was irony. The giant was gruff and no one heard a sound.

The three that remain in the dining room are fully impressed, it couldn't have gotten off to a better start. David had been apprehensive, his nerves jittery before all this – and the hangover hadn't helped – but he had to admit, Ben's manners have been exquisite, his demeanour surprising, but surprisingly positive, almost inspiring.

In the living room Ben snatches his satchel from the side of the couch. The room is dim, the curtains open and night is approaching fast. Winter. Always upon you. Every time you look outside it is either cold or wet or dark, few variables. Ben likes the summer months when the light is strong and the days stretch, days stretch so far they turn into memories of longer days, as a boy, running, two taller boys beside him, hurley sticks, a football, a dog barking wildly, chained up and dying to take part in the fun but too dangerous to be let loose.

Ben, also too dangerous to be let loose.

But here he is now, in a stranger's house, a stranger's room.

He takes out the envelope he'd received from the man in the van, as well as the promised bottle of wine – a good bottle that he paid extra for, more than he normally would. A better choice, for *better* people ... but better than *who*?

He goes to the drinks cabinet and finds the corkscrew that had caused Charles such trouble. He admires its twisty-to-a-point shape, such marvellous engineering, and such convenience, when you knew how of course, when you had the strength to push it in correctly, twist and pull, pull, pull out the very heart of the thing to reveal the secrets inside.

He glances once more at the art on the walls as he heads back to the dining room. They are proud of their pictures, their *objets*, and why wouldn't they be? If you have these things you may as well show them off. Every visitor to this house is sure to remark on them, and surely Charles takes great pride in outlining their history, these gifts, tokens of appreciation, souvenirs, awards. And that Lucian Freud one, yes, that is worth a few quid, no doubt about it. Ben knows a man in Amsterdam who'd be more than happy to come across such a thing. There has to be even more of this stuff upstairs, there simply must.

When Ben returns to the family dinner the others are happily chatting, happily chewing. Lydia's meal is going down very well and even though they have broken tradition – having it on the Eve and not the Day – no one is complaining.

Lydia sees the bottle in his hand and, quite obviously tipsy now, is keen to offer her appreciation:

"Oh, how nice of you. Thank you, sweetheart."

The endearments get thrown around so easily here. *Sweetheart. Darling. Son.* For a moment he almost feels like he belongs. But he won't allow himself that. He has never belonged anywhere, except between the pillars of his two loyal accomplices. Only there. Safe. Assured.

"No worries," Ben says, "now, give me your glasses."

Lydia speaks to her son in pretend-whisper, expecting to be heard:

"A fine catch there, David. I'm sure he takes care of you very well."

Ben smiles. Yes. He does. He takes care of everything very well. He plans. He wraps. He even puts little bows and ribbons on things. Very gay. But it's what people expect. You don't want to let people down, now do you?

He takes their glasses from them and puts them on the side table with his back to them. He could be a bartender. He could be a servant from a bygone era in a stately home, he could be a landlord's aide, a butler. Class. England never gets over it.

"It is we that should be doing the serving, Ben. You're the guest."

There is that sonorous voice again. The one that can reach to the back rows of the theatre. Straight from the diaphragm, the throat under no strain at all. Dulcet tones. *Dulcet*: that was another one of those phrases for such voices that not only ran deep, but was also somehow euphonious, as if – because you have heard it so many times before in TV commercials, voiceovers – that it was somehow charming. *Dulcet*. Canorous. It is a wonderful weapon indeed to have in your arsenal, especially when you are bending someone to do your bidding.

Ben carries on, unscrewing the cork from this bottle. Again he does this with such aplomb, pouring a good wine into their good glasses.

As the family chat idly about cranberry sauce, about the lifelike figures in the local church's crib, about not bothering to get a real tree next time and get one good solid artificial one instead to see them out for the rest of their days, Ben takes out three pills from the envelope in his pocket without anyone noticing. He pops one pill into each of their glasses. Mama bear, Papa bear, Baby bear, too. But not his own. Not Ben. Not this Goldilocks. He needs to stay on the outside. Goldilocks needs to stay awake for it all. For the fairy-tale fireworks. If things are to go according...

He turns around to face them and this Goldilocks has morphed into the wicked wolf – Ben has a great grin stretching across his face and is delighted to hand them out their glasses. Delighted to serve them. Class.

They raise them aloft and toast yet again. What a day. What a wonderful day it is turning out to be. A roaring success. One of the best Christmases the Cunninghams had in a long time – David hadn't even made it home the previous year, had decided to stay in the city, partying it out there, with his new lover, the dark, mysterious, brooding lover. This is far better. Christmas: a family occasion. Time for giving and receiving. And to think they had all been nervous about it. The first meeting. The boyfriend introduced to the parents for the first time. What was to be nervous about? It is all going swimmingly. A fine catch.

"I didn't know about the wine, honestly," says David. "But I do know that he has one more trick up his sleeve, isn't that right, hon?"

Ben looks alarmed for a split second until he realises what David is referring to.

"The crackers! Yes. Of course!"

"Crackers?" says Charles, clearly intrigued and already rising to the prospect of theatricality. You never knew what would happen in this second act. A great playwright always keeps things back, gives out little breadcrumby clues, alludes to things that may or may not show up. Ben is today's expert dramatist, throwing a few morsels along the trail, and the audience picks them up, hungrily, curiously, and they follow him, they always follow him, his introverted nature somehow magnetic, pulling in those around him, daring them to try and unveil, and try to crack his code: the crux of the allure.

"Crackers?" says Charles again, his smile wide and childish. "Whatever could that be all about?"

"Just wait and see," teases Ben. "You'll just have to wait and see."

18

A white van pulls into the car park of an American-style retro fast-food place. A few seconds later its white twin pulls right up alongside it.

The burly brothers get out of their vehicles, banging their doors shut in synchronicity and sending a couple of scavenging crows back into the blackening sky. They walk with long strides, long arms hanging by their sides; the whole thing could be choreographed for a rock video, or for the opening of a gangster movie.

Brick wears black.

Brac wears a dark shade of red.

Brick's cobra eyes are a different colour from the cobra eyes at the side of Brac's equally thick neck, but almost everything else about them is the same: body size, body shape, the disappointed expressions on their faces as they consider the tacky decorations of the premises. Is this place being purposely tasteless? Some sort of irony at play here? Awful plastic Santas and snowmen. Dirty fake snow on the smeared windows. Tasteless. Not a word you want in your mind as you head into a restaurant, fast-food joint or otherwise, the place could do with a rethink, or a dirty bomb.

Brick Herbert opens the door and allows his younger-by-ten-minutes brother to enter. Elton John's "Step Into

Christmas" is playing loudly but they are prepared to give Elton a pass. He's been around a long time and as far as they know hasn't diddled any minors, so that's something. The rhythm of the song is not half bad, there's a sense of propulsion about it, a nice clear bass line that manages to be melodic as well as rhythmic. For the brothers, it'll do.

They stand side by side, these mountains of men, large and imposing. You cannot but notice them.

As they stare up at the overhead board menu deciding on their choice of food, the teenage server from behind the counter looks straight at them, from one face to the other, surprised, amused, it's almost as if she is trying to spot differences, it could be a round in a game show.

The brothers take their eyes off the board at the same moment and glare hard at her. The young girl's amusement quickly dissipates and she stutters out a welcome.

They sit at a table munching into their hamburgers. They eat quickly and without any apparent joy. They are hungry. They are always hungry. They work out a lot, and really shouldn't be pushing such junk into their bodies. But they are on a job today and don't have much time. They'll get the chance over the next few days to burn off all those calories. They'll punish themselves.

They eat in silence, barely making eye contact. Every so often one of them takes a napkin and wipes away the gunk from the corner his mouth, but not a word, not a single syllable out of either of them.

When they are finished Brick takes an envelope out of his pocket and slides it across the table to his brother.

Brac picks it up and reads: *Charles Cunningham, 62, renowned actor. Address, Poplar Drive.*

Brick's face brightens further at what he reads next. *Items: paintings, objets d'art, theatre posters and memorabilia, jewellery – valuable? wine cellar?*

He hands the note back to his twin, the job clearer in his head now, real things, easy to visualise.

Brick balls up the note and mixes it in with the hamburger wrapper and the ketchup-stained napkins, no one will ever fish that out.

They take out their phones and swap information quickly, silently. *1957.* They hit delete on all previous emails and wipe their phones clean and get ready to go.

The spotty young server watches them as they carry their trays to the rubbish receptacles and put all their waste in the correct places – paper in the paper hole, ice-dregs swirling down the funnelled chute. They place their trays neatly on top of one another.

Brick knows he is being watched. He turns and winks at the nervy server, she smiles a tremulous smile back at him.

They strut out of the restaurant wincing at the bad decorations, glad to leave them behind. They have grown used to good art, have even developed a taste for it – they've certainly stolen enough of it over the years. They have learned to tell what is worth something and what is worth fuck all. They have read up on the subjects: paintings, sketches, sculpture; scoured online articles to bring themselves up to speed with the ever-changing art world and its gluttonous markets. They have educated themselves. Rewards, they reap.

Outside, they stand and gaze out along the car park. They check to see if anybody has clocked them. It would be best not to be seen at all this day. Luckily most people are embroiled in their own Christmas cocoons, stocking up, buying last-minute guilty gifts – for two normally noticeable men then they'll get away with anything today.

They take out their vaping accoutrements, quickly prepare and in no time are exhaling in unison to the frosty air. A few spatters of rain fall, but no showers yet, and though hatless, scarf-less, they feel not a prick of cold. They stand there vacant and vaping.

Back in their vans they reverse in opposite directions first then drive away, one after the other, ten-minute older brother leading the way for ten-minute younger brother. It could all indeed be choreographed. A kind of gritty urban ballet, ballet of bulk.

They are on their way.

They are on their way to work.

A job is a job and they are never late.

And they never ever let down their mate.

19

Ben has eaten as much as was polite and is now standing with his satchel over his shoulder, a wrapped box under his arm. He listens to the family conversation and watches Charles Cunningham pat his rotundity.

"I can hardly move. I'll need a forklift to get me up the stairs tonight."

Lydia, further along in her drunkenness, addresses them all.

"I hope you have kept a bit of room for the plum pudding. Christmas wouldn't be the same without it."

"I think I'd prefer my marshmallows to be honest."

"Marshmallows?" says David, incredulous. "Do explain, Pater. Is this all a precursor to senility?"

"Look, I was just saying that they are so easy to eat. What was the word I used earlier? *Insignificant.* They're just so insignificant. They take no effort. You just put them into your mouth and hardly even chew and they just disappear. I find the whole process, I don't know, comforting. Maybe it's because I'm getting old and chewing is like … remember that dish we had last week, that Greek restaurant we went to …"

"Yes," says Lydia, trying to supress a yawn; she is suddenly exceedingly sleepy. "We were practising. Getting ready for the trip. You had the calamari."

"Calamari! That's the one! I thought I'd never get through it, the squid or octopus or whatever it was, it was so bloody chewy. My jaws were aching after it. How comforting it is to have something soft and easy. Not hard, not something that fights back."

He is laughing now but no one else joins in with him.

"Marshmallows. They just disappear. So soon forgotten."

Ben feels like he could run. He feels like he should be out on the night streets, running, regardless of rain or the sheets of sleet that are expected, his limbs screaming with pain as he pushes them harder and harder, dopamine running through him, endorphins, the pleasure of physical exercise, its reward. He feels stiff and useless here looking down on them, a family at a family table, and this monologue, this preposterous speech…

Ben's heart is racing, and he is not moving at all.

"That's just plain weird," says David. "Mid-life crisis I'd say but you're well beyond that."

His father laughs, "Maybe it is weird. But they remind me of my childhood. Easy days. Sweet and soft and good."

Ben looks at the clock on the wall, he's growing impatient now. It is twenty minutes to six. He rattles the box playfully to get everyone's attention.

"Is this the mystery we've been waiting for?" Charles is also trying to stifle a yawn. "These are the crackers then?"

Ben hands the box to Lydia and she tries to engage with it but her eyes are getting more glazed by the minute; she can't believe that it's so early in the evening and already her bed is beckoning.

"Almost a shame to open it," she says. "The wrapping looks so lovely. You went to such an effort."

"He always wraps things up very well," says David.

"I just like putting things into position. Setting the scene, you know."

"It's funny we haven't come across each other before," says Charles, still patting his bloated stomach. A dreadful tiredness has come over him too. What is it about turkey that makes one so sleepy? He read about it just the other week, some chemical...he can't remember what it's called.

"Go ahead now," says Ben. "Why don't you open it?"

Lydia just about manages to tear the wrapping from the box and extract the box of crackers.

"Beautiful," she says.

"All his own handiwork," says David through yet another yawn.

"I bought the kit online and assembled them myself."

"I always thought they were a kind of stupid tradition," says Charles. "Pulling crackers. How did such a thing ever come about?"

"They were originally called *cosaques*, which probably came from *Cossack*, because those guys liked to go around firing guns into the air as they rode about on horses."

David's next yawn is wide and gaping but it doesn't stop Ben from continuing – he doesn't mind one bit if his story is soporific; ironically, it might only accelerate his evening.

"A sweet maker named Tom Smith is said to be the first guy to have made these kind of crackers, in about 1850. He liked to have fancy wrapping on his sweets and would include little riddles inside the wrappings to amuse children. They say one night, while he was looking at an open fire, he got the idea that his sweet wrappings should crackle or snap too, when opened, you know, to make it exciting for children. Thus the idea was born."

He could be a boring tour guide in a museum, a dull professor of History in some ill-attended university: David is wondering why he is talking so much. He never talks this much! What has come over him? In the morning he hardly said a word, just grunted and grumbled. Maybe he had snorted something when he left the room a few minutes ago; David could do with a snort of something himself because he is fading fast.

"Sorry, am I boring everyone?"

"Yes," says David. "This is why I try to get him to go out more. Instead of staying at home every night reading Wikipedia. He reads the most random stuff. Once I even found him looking at a website on how to make homemade bombs."

The others are too sleepy to look startled.

"It was for a play. Props. Just wanted to make them look authentic."

"I like the story of the crackers," says Charles. "You are very wise. That's us! The three wise men at Christmas. And one woman of course."

Lydia doesn't have the energy to roll her eyes but she does support her husband.

"Yes, very interesting, Ben. We learn something new every day. What harm is a bit of knowledge? The Internet should be more than just pornography and people shouting obscenities at each other on Tweeter."

"Twitter," corrects David.

"Whatever. You know what I mean."

Charles takes a big gulp of his wine. His mouth has gone very dry but still he manages:

"I agree, my love. If you are going to read – and no one reads books anymore, bloody libraries closing down all over the country – why not read something interesting?"

"Agreed," says Ben, looking pleasingly around at the sight of three bodies fairly crumpling on the seats before him. David in particular looks like he is seconds away from sleep and apologising to everyone for his sudden sleepiness.

Ben defends, "He had a rough night last night. And then the long drive. It takes a lot out of you."

Lydia is still holding the box of crackers.

"I'm going to try one. Who'll pull it with me?"

"I will," says Charles, trying to summon some energy, "Are there hats inside too?"

"Of course," says Ben.

Lydia and Charles hold each end of the cracker.

"Ready?" he asks.

"Ready when you are."

"OK, one, two, three ..."

20

Although Brac Herbert doesn't wish it could be Christmas every day, he knows it can be a very fruitful time. He knows many people are so preoccupied that they become vulnerable; there are many last-minute bargains to be had; Brac and brother Brick are the types who'll gladly provide to anyone who comes knocking.

The kids can start singing and the band can play as much as they bloody well want, it won't derail Brac Herbert. He stays focused, he doesn't even whistle along to that tune as it plays in the van now. Roy Wood and Wizzard. And the kids in the chorus. He wonders if they got any royalties too, or did it all go into Roy Wood's pocket. And Wizzard's. A video like that would be fucking dodgy these days: grizzled long-bearded geezer hanging round a load of schoolkids, alarm bells would be ringing straight away, not Christmas bells. These are the times Brac lives in. There was plenty of it about back in his day, plenty of wrong 'uns who would visit the orphanage and slip their hands into your pockets and ask if you had any money for sweeties – they might pop a ten-pence piece in for your troubles, but only after a little rummage around first.

Brick Herbert is not listening to the same song as he drives in the other van. He's still got the Sleaford Mods going. Relentless beats. Spat-out lyrics. You can watch clips of the singer on YouTube – maybe it's from Glastonbury – and the camera is up quite close on the singer, and there are sprays of spit just leaping out of his mouth. Top bloke that fella. No one's clown. Says it like it is. No messing about. Gotta take your hat off to blokes like that. He'd go see 'em, the pair of 'em, if they were playing anywhere near. Likes a good mosh up at the front of the stage, does Brick.

So does Brac.

But they are driving now.

They are on the job. They might be thinking about music and dodgy blokes and top blokes but that does not mean they are not focused on their task. They are. They have a job to do and they're bang on time. They'll be at their destination soon enough. Their spirits are high. Their blood up.

The streets are wetter now. Drops of rain. Nothing heavy yet. No snow. The weather forecast said fuck-all chance of that. Cold though. It's a bit nippy so they drive with their heating on. Not the best season to be a skinhead, but they'll be busy soon enough and will keep warm. Moving things around. Moving, moving, always on the go, these lads. Loading up. Loading up the two white vans. And not a pig in sight. Often they'd be out these times with the breathalysers checking up on the drunk drivers, idiots who've had one too many at the office party and foolishly take the car home. Careless. Stupid cunts, really. Risky business with the feds around. Brick and Brac don't even drink anymore. It just slows them down. They'd rather gulp down the whey protein every day. Build themselves up. Build themselves right the fuck up. The more you build yourself up the less chance you have of being knocked down. There's a logic to that. Makes sense. They like things that make sense. Simple equations.

They are driving now.

They do not go over the speed limit. Not with so much at stake. They are careful and controlled and they know exactly what they are doing.

Synchronised.

Since their first minutes together, out into the world and silent.

What's to say?

Same instincts: same drives.

They carry on.

21

A whip cracks loudly on the empty stage. Pozzo is practising whipping the floor. He is dressed the part, this
actor, yes, he is very convincing, his look, his movements,
you would have no trouble at all believing he is the master
and he can get his slave to do what he requires. He's got the
haughtiness down pat, the anger and arrogance, the look of
despotism that dangles under those bushy eyebrows.

The skinny director walks on to the stage to join
him. He has to stand well back lest the whip fly out and
accidentally catch him. It is a prop, sure, but it is real
enough to do damage. He had made sure to get a better
one, as requested, the best available; he bends for this actor,
this man of prestige, actor of renown, many bend to his
will, to his hauteur.

"We're done for the day. I'm turning the lights out.
Early start tomorrow. Go get some rest. Be with that lovely
wife of yours," the director says.

"Sure," says Pozzo, in the voice of Pozzo, still believing
himself to be Pozzo and not someone else, he's not himself.
He finds it pleasurable to stay as Beckett's bumptious boor,
and he carries that whip so well. He finds pleasure in the
praise, the raise of the stage, people looking at him, liking

what he does, liking his craft. He has no problems with any of this, is in complete control.

He cracks the whip once more across the boards, expertly. He is used to using it now, he could be a lion tamer, and the director steps even further back, lest lashes land.

"I'm very happy with this," Pozzo says.

"Good," says the director, pleased to appease.

"And the rope is not bad either. Finally."

"Good," says the director again, tired after a long day's rehearsals and wanting to be out of there, wanting to be relaxing at home, a glass of red wine, maybe a bath and an early night.

"So many instruments of torture."

"C'mon, off with you now, my good man. You'll need rest for tomorrow. Busy day."

"Has everyone else gone?"

"It's just the lad left, backstage. You said you'd drop him back to the foster home, yeah?"

"Of course, yeah. No problem. I have my car."

"He's with a different family to the last time."

"Who's he with now? Where do I take him?"

"He'll let you know. He has the address written down."

"Fine," says Pozzo. "Goodnight then."

He watches the director depart, white ponytail swinging behind him.

"And behave yourself!" shouts the director, without turning his back.

"Naturally," says Pozzo. But maybe it is not the voice of Pozzo this time, maybe it is his own, real voice, deep, coming from somewhere deep down, "Naturally."

22

The cracker snaps loudly and both Charles and Lydia are surprised at the sound – they've never heard a cracker sound so loud before.

It even wakes David up. Had he drifted off? He closed his eyes there for just one second and…what the hell is wrong with him? Last night had been a pretty heavy one, but he's never felt this exhausted before, all his muscles seem to be sagging on him, the life draining out of him, as if a suction pump has been attached and is extracting all his energy. Is he sick? Is that it? Is he so rundown that he is becoming ill?

Charles is yawning too, even as he puts the paper party hat on and declares himself king. He tells Lydia again that he would make a great Lear and she is too tired now to argue. Fuck it: if he wants to have another ten years on the stage then let him have it, let him collapse and die there, what can she do about it? He is a stubborn old mule at the best of times…although now that she comes to think of it they'll probably not even want him. The theatre company. Whichever one it is. Any theatre company! Why would they want him? He can hardly remember anything these days, has become so absent-minded and…Jesus fuck but she's drunk too much this day, she's just realised this now, she's drunker than she thought she was, she shouldn't have bothered with that early sherry, and she's necked down some of that red wine and all, she's bloody pissed now and fracturing with fatigue.

"You certainly got the snap into it, Ben," says Charles. "Well done, lad. Some of the ones you'd buy in the shops, you'd pull them and expect a great snap and ... nothing, nothing at all. Such disappointment. And the useless little trinkets they put inside. And the moronic jokes."

Charles positions the hat better on his head.

"Do I look regal enough: *O Lear, Lear, Lear!*"

He strikes at his own head.

"*Beat at this gate, that let thy folly in, and thy dear judgement out! – Go, go, my people.*"

"Marvellous," says Ben clapping wildly and Charles takes an exaggerated bow.

David and his mother look like they are in a competition to see who can yawn the widest. They could be two hippos at a watering hole, lazy in the hot sub-Saharan sun.

But this is winter.

And this is England.

And this is no good at all. Yawning is contagious and Ben has to look away or he'll be drawn in too.

"Aren't you going to read the instruction?"

"Instruction? There's no joke?"

"No," says Ben, "this is more of a game kind of thing. That's the surprise! If you'll play along ..."

Charles feels very tired, awfully tired in fact, but he decides he will, he'll give it a go, it is Christmas after all, a time for family and joyful parlour games, he can rise to the challenge, when has he ever not? What harm a bit of nonsense? Christmas after all. A time for ...

He doesn't even notice that his wife and son are completely out for the count.

"You're a card all right," he says to Ben. "Full of tricks!"

Charles is smiling as he picks up the paper that has fallen out of the cracker.

"Wait, hang on," he says. "I need my glasses."

Ben sighs impatiently, keeping a close eye on the clock on the wall.

Charles finds his spectacles from the table at the side of the room and puts them on. It's only then that he notices the other two sound asleep.

"Well, would you look at the state of those two! Not going to be much of a game if they're not going to take part."

He puts on his glasses and reads aloud from the slip of paper, yet another look of confusion coming over him.

"At precisely six o'clock look out the living room window."

The glasses are perched on the end of his nose and he looks out from over them, straight into Ben's unflinching eyes.

"I don't get it."

He looks at the sleeping couple, irritation spreading through his veins.

"For heaven's sake, Lydia! David! Wake up! We're just starting a game!"

The sleeping couple does not respond; Charles himself lets out a big, gaping yawn.

"I'm actually feeling pretty tired myself, son. Exhausted all of a sudden. Perhaps the excitement you know, your visit and..."

He doesn't have the energy to finish his sentence.

"Let's just continue the game, Mr. Cunningham. *Charles.* Let's think of it as a warm-up exercise at the beginning of a drama class."

"Yes, yes," says Charles slightly reeling, but trying to be a good sport nevertheless, attempting as ever to be liked, to win over.

Ben takes Charles by the arm and gently motions him to move out of the room. Charles moves obediently, his body feeling extremely heavy now, he is hardly able to push one foot in front of the other. Age, the autumn of one's life... or is it now winter... who'd have it?

In the living room Ben asks him to read the piece of paper again.

"Six o'clock," says Charles. "Six o'clock it says."

"Then look out."

Charles looks out the window into the dark night.

Ben pulls the plug on the fairy lights to allow him a better view, "Can you see anything out there?"

Outside the house the lights of two white vans flash once. Then flash again.

"Yes, yes, there are two vans out there. Go wake David up. Tell him the game..."

Charles takes a staggering step back and collapses on the sofa.

"Yes," says Ben, "the game."

Ben's stomach has started to tremble with excitement. This is what he has been waiting for. After all this time.

Charles' eyes have shut completely and he is slumped now and snoring.

A few minutes later two tall muscular men stand on either side of Ben Morrigan, towering and tough.

Ben smiles, comfortable between them, safe, feeling a little at home, at last.

"We've got work to do," he says.

The two brothers nod and spring into action.

All Brick's Christmases seem to have come at once. He is looking around at the art on the walls, the sculptures on the mini podiums, his eyes are wide and avaricious. But he has to move fast. Everything about this evening is about speed, efficiency. No time to waste. They can only sleep so long, the two in the dining room. The drug will wear off eventually. They will wake up and then they will scream to the high heavens.

His brother starts to tie up the sleeping mother and son to their chairs. He even thinks about tying them together, mother and son, a nativity scene, her cradling him, this infant so tender and mild, sleeping in heavenly ... but there is no time to be creative, no time for faffing about. The job needs to be done. His stomach flutters with a giddy excitement too.

All three mount the stairs with terrific strides and enter Charles' office. There is a desk with an Anglepoise lamp and a laptop on top of it. There are theatre pictures and posters adorning the walls. Naturally the brothers begin to collect every last one of them, careful not to tear – despite their speed they are tender, they know what things are worth.

Behind the desk there is a safe and Ben bends to it.

"I'm going to take a chance here, but if this cunt is as dumb as I think he is, then we already know the combination."

Ben turns the dial: 1-9-5-7... and the thing actually opens.

"The poor fucker's memory is shot. He has to keep things simple."

Ben greedily grabs wads of cash, envelopes and other business documents. He turns to Brac and hands them over.

"Bag all this stuff. We can sort it out later."

He holds two passports in his hands, examines them, then sticks them back in the safe.

Brick gives him a quizzical look.

"Just leave those."

With great haste the brothers bring their loot to one of the open vans. They load in paintings, posters, statuettes, and any reasonably-sized furniture they think might make some cash. They have been in enough houses to know what has value and what is trash. This is not an Ikea kind of house, the things they take will be easy to offload, easy money. They slog until one of the vans is full to capacity. A good night's work. Well done, chaps.

Ben takes the Silencerco Osprey 9mm silencer from his satchel and attaches it to his piece. The last thing he wants is for Charles to wake up now and for him to have to actually use it – blood the last thing you need on an occasion like this, a fat body to dispose of even worse – but he has to consider the possibility. Charles is a large man, and could be rash and could be more trouble than he expects, you never know with a cornered animal... but when Ben enters the living room Charles is still sleeping soundly, whatever foolish dreams he is having. Maybe about marshmallows. The dopey cunt.

The brothers appear behind their leader.

"Get him in the van. Make sure he's gagged."

They lift him off the sofa and drag him out into the hallway and out the door. They bundle him into the van – Brick climbing in after him and tying his hands tightly behind his back.

Ben oversees the operation and stands at the doorway looking out across the wide grounds and the lights of neighbouring houses. Everyone must be so involved in their Christmas Eve celebrations that no one is watching them. They'll have their boxes of chocolates on their coffee tables in front of them. They'll have the telly on and will be knocking back cans of lager and glasses of Baileys and not bothering one jot about what is happening outside. Society could be descending into chaos right outside, a zombie apocalypse could be upon them, but it won't distract them from siphoning every minute of the Yuletide fare. Logs on the fire. Gifts on the trees. It's the perfect time for getting a proper job done without any busybody sticking their fucking nose in.

Ben returns to the house, returns to the dining room.

Lydia and David are tied to their chairs – no chance of getting out of those binds. When he sees them he feels a momentary pang of regret. This is the man he shared a bed with, for months. He had fondled him. Ben shudders. Most of all, he had lied to him.

The pang of regret does not last long; there's no backing out now.

He takes out a pair of thin gloves from his satchel and puts them on. Then he takes out an envelope from the same bag and places it on the dining-room table in front of the knocked-out couple.

The lines of the letter echo in his head as he continues his work.

David, follow my instructions carefully. Someone will be here soon to untie you.

He looks around the dining room. He takes a napkin with a snowman motif from the side table and begins to wipe down surfaces.

Your father has one last opportunity, for his greatest, most honest performance ever.

He wipes down the fork and knife that he had used.

Do not contact the police. If you do, you will find yourselves in grave danger.

He remembers composing this. "Grave", not "great". It had more resonance.

He wipes down the wine glass he drank from.

I know everything about your life, remember, and you know nothing about me.

He wipes the glasses the others drank from because he had held them.

Do not underestimate me.

He had written this twice.

Do not underestimate me.

He wipes the bottle that he had uncorked.

This was the only way – it had to be done. Someday you will understand.

He wipes around the table where he had sat and the back of the chair and any other thing he thought his fingers might have brushed against.

You will never see or hear from me again.

He had thought about writing "Merry Christmas" but thought better of it, one can only go so far.

He goes back to the living room and wipes down as much as he can there, too. Surfaces, surfaces, wherever his hands may have been.

Before he leaves the room he takes one more look at the Christmas tree Charles had erected. Yes, it does indeed look crooked. It was an obvious metaphor, standing there, crooked, tall, imposing, but wrong, and then the strangest thing happens, just as Ben is thinking all this, the tree, perhaps unable to take any more of the strain, perhaps no longer able to withstand the pressure, leans forward and topples clumsily to the floor. Although Ben is startled, he cannot help but burst into a manic and somehow relieved laughter. Everything is working out perfectly. Even better than expected. The Christmas you get…

In the rear-view mirror Ben can see the open door of the Cunningham house and the inviting light of the hallway.

"Rocking Around the Christmas Tree" comes on the van stereo system and Ben groans.

"Jesus Christ. You got any proper music?"

Brac nods in the direction of the glove compartment and Ben takes out a Sleaford Mods CD.

"Army Nights" starts up. That's more like it.

Sounds come from the back of the van as Charles – already waking? – shuffles around. He may be frightened and he may be sore and cold, but both Ben and Brac couldn't give a shit either way, they are enjoying the Sleaford's brutal take on life – they just crank the cracking tune up louder; the old man can kick and scream all the fuck he wants, no one that cares will ever hear.

They hurtle on.

The quiet roads.

Not a soul abroad.

Beats in the front of the van.

Bleats from the back of the van – Charles is gagged of course, for the first time in his life, this actor, no one can hear what he has to say.

23

A busy pub chock-full of Christmas revellers. Many are standing at the bar shout-ordering; some are at tables with glasses of various sizes in front of them: pints, halves, whiskies, shots. A flaming Sambuca illuminates one of the tables but the drink is soon quenched and downed. One adventurous partygoer climbs a sticky table when the opening notes of "Fairytale Of New York" start up, but a pair of burly bouncers are quick to the scene and coax him down in as restrained a manner as they can manage – they could be tested once or twice more this evening, but so far tempers are tame.

Janie has seen things kick off in such pubs before, it only takes one stupid action, a passing touch on a bare arm, a remark after a testy local derby, often it takes very little at all to get things up and fuming, but so far everyone here seems to be having fun and the table-top tinsel-wrapped trickster is soon settled again, glugging back on his pint of lager, embarrassed that his friends have captured the moment to live on the Internet for all eternity.

Janie and Patrick are the mildest couple in the bar, more like spectators watching the proceedings, aloof from it all, but enjoying it nonetheless.

"Place is buzzing," says Patrick, never having remembered this particular establishment being so busy before. Perhaps people are out to forget about the political worries that bombard their TV screens, the protests, the threats and catastrophes – at Christmas you can put things aside for a week or so, and the people in delirious decadence before them are the perfect proponents.

"Christmas Eve," sighs Janie. "People aren't pissed enough yet to go home and face their families."

She had a point. Political and environmental disasters were one thing, but Christmas with the family was equally imminent and equally unavoidable.

Janie says she's pleased they got out early and jokes that it must be the nearest thing they'll get to a bonus this year.

Patrick has to agree, "That's as good as it gets I'm afraid, my dear … when you've known him as long as I have. But wait till he hears about the broken security cameras."

"He'll go fucking ape."

"Probably. But fuck it. He's got money enough to fix it, it's not like he's short of a bob or two … like the rest of us."

Janie only ever took the job to pay off student loans, but two years later she's still there, and still deep in debt. Her mother, suffering from depression, doesn't help matters; Janie has a lot to be getting on with, none of it easy. She has kept her sights on training to be a criminal psychologist – she has kept her sights on many things that haven't yet panned out – but she is trying to see off this year in an optimistic fashion, hoping the next one will bear more fruit.

"Father Christmas coming to the kids tonight?"

"Course, he is," says Patrick. "Presents are all wrapped up and sitting under the tree. I don't even know what they are to be honest; the wife takes care of all that. Your shopping all done?"

"Yup," she says lifting her glass to her lips. "Gonna head home after this one. Spend the night with Mum. You know how it is."

"How's she doing?"

"Same. Ups and downs. She likes Christmas though, lots on the telly to keep her occupied."

"Do give her my love."

"I will, Pat, cheers."

They clink glasses.

They both survey the Christmas chaos, the bellicose choruses, the sways, the hugs and sloppy, slobbering kisses.

"I'll have a few drinks tomorrow to make up for it. There's always a bottle of Baileys in the house."

Janie takes out her phone, checks her messages then puts it on the table in front of her. She checks on it regularly to see if her mother is needing any help. When the hip operation went wrong and caused even more damage than was there in the first place, it only added to her mental fragility – Janie is forever on red alert, ever wary, very tired.

She sees the Christmas cracker lying there in the crater of her open bag, the one she got from the strange guy who had stopped for petrol.

"I'd forgotten about that."

She takes it out to examine it again.

"All a bit strange, wasn't it, those lads," says Patrick. "Still, nice gesture I suppose. Better than the sour pusses you get from some folk these days. Not even a thank you and you after wiping their shitty windscreens for them."

"All part of the service."

"You're still young enough to go and find yourself a decent job. With your qualifications and all."

"All in good time, Pat. All in good time. A few more debts to pay off... but we're getting there."

Patrick takes a drink from his pint of Guinness. It's his normal tipple, the legacy passed on from his Irish father, a Kilburn regular and self-proclaimed expert on porter, and although this isn't one of the Irish pubs he usually frequents, they served it up pretty well in his opinion, the head of it creamy, the body full, the temperature right, the lads here seemed to have nailed it, even on a busy night like this when patience is in short supply and everyone is baying for more.

"Aren't you going to pull it then? The cracker?"

"It takes two to pull," she tells him.

"Ha, there's a line and a half."

"The bloke said I wasn't supposed to pull it till nine o'clock."

"Playing some kind of mind games or something, was he?"

"Who knows? Never saw the guy before."

She muses for a second before adding, "Was kind of sexy though."

"And gay."

"Well... maybe."

"*Maybe?* He was as bent as a ..."

"Go on, finish it."

"We're not allowed say those kinds of things anymore. The PC brigade... you know the story. I'll be all over the newspapers before you know it. Some sneaky cunt will catch me on their phone. I'll be gone viral!"

"You know you're not allowed say *cunt* either?"

Patrick erupts with a laugh, nearly choking on his pint, and has to disgustingly spit some of it back into the glass.

"Cunt is one of the great British words. It all depends on the intonation. And who you are saying it to. We haven't become completely American yet."

"I'll take your word for it."

"Go on then, let's pull the bloody thing. See what stupid jokes are inside," Patrick checks his watch as he says this. "It's quarter to nine. Close enough. Come on, I've got to get home and pretend to be sober."

The previous table-topper is trying his luck again, but the bouncers have had enough of him and are escorting him to the door. He's complaining that he hasn't got his jacket with him but the two big men seem to have little compassion. They take the sloshing glass from his hand and put it on a nearby table and then drag him through the parting crowd to the exit.

Janie is more focused on the Christmas cracker.

"Seems a shame to pull it. It seems so well crafted."

"For fuck's sake, you could say the same about your egg in the morning, but you still crack it open and dip in your soldiers."

"Soldiers! Jesus Christ, I haven't heard that in years!"

She holds out the cracker to him and he takes the other end of it.

"You ready?" she asks. "OK, one, two, three…"

ACT III

24

Wakes.
He wakes up.

Wakefulness? Is that what this is? Is this life... still? Perhaps it is a concussion? He's never had one before, this could be it?

Con-cuss-ion.

The word sounds and rebounds in his own head, sounds like percussion.

Per-cuss-ion.

There is rhythm. Is it the flow of blood in his brain that creates it? He can hear practically nothing else. It is so very quiet where he is. Just the beat of his blood. His heart. Where is he?

Things swirl: Memories recent. Memories old. Memories hot. Memories cold. Memories fraught. Memories bold. Some memories rot and some memories scold.

That's Bach being played by Glenn Gould, in his head now. When was that? At his home? Is that when that was? Someone... someone was coming to visit him in his home. A guest. He was expecting a guest.

Sherry. He seems to remember sherry. Someone was drinking sherry. Those little glasses. Lydia. Merry. Of course. He has been married to her for years. Merry. Married. Years.

Millions of years, ha, that was the joke. He remembers that now. Sherry and jokes and eye-rolls. A new dress. Where is she? And there was…something about Pinter. Harold Pinter, the playwright. Or was it a book about Beckett? It's all mixed-up now in the throb of his head. It is all so perplexing. He feels like he's losing.

Lear! He will play the part of King Lear! Has he already auditioned for this? He played Prospero too, played Spooner and…

He feels groggy, is it a concussion? Is that what this is? He's never had one before, could this be it? Or is he dead? Surely not. The beat of blood, the heart still beating too. If not dead then moribund at the very least; a Beckett character on a bare stage, the voices around him…the voices are his own…in his own head. The worst prison of all. Is this some kind of play? Is that what's going on here?

Memories old. Memories scold.

You don't know what those poor boys have been subjected to.

What?

Who said that? Where did that voice come from?

Wells.

Wells within.

Wells.

Swells.

Con-cuss-ion.

Per-cuss-ion.

Maybe I should write one. A play about just that. My younger, wilder days. Days of secret savagery. I'll call it Marshmallows. Not a bad idea, actually.

What?

Who said that?

Prison head. And it throbs. What had he taken?

Caliginous. This is a word that comes to him now, with his eyes shut and the rhythms of blood in body, beating around his body, beating around his beat-up body. *Caliginous.* It means dim, dark, murky, misty, obscure. He must have come across that word somewhere. What an odd word to spring from nowhere.

This is how he feels. Caliginous. Had it been a crossword clue? He has never been any good at those, especially the cryptic ones. He never got them. He is much more literal than that. The script always tells him what to do. Follow the directions.

Caliginous.

Dark.

Shadowy.

Where could he be? If he is not dead then he must very well be alive. Stands to reason. Blood. Heart. And if he is alive then he must be someplace. Some *place.*

Where is this place?

Spooner. He had played Spooner. That wasn't so long ago. Something about memory, that drama, and there was a photo album as part of the plot – was it a prop, or did they only discuss the photo album? And who was the other character? Hirst. Hirst. Wasn't it? And there was a photo album right there beside him on the sofa. His son, on Santa's lap.

Dodgy, those blokes.

He struggles to open his eyes.

Oh, look, we're not getting into all that again.

They are only half-open, like they have been glued shut, is that from his own tears, or has blood welled there? Welled. His eyes swelled. Has he been beaten, or has that yet to come? For some reason he feels it looms. A beating. A beating looms. His gut tells him this. Maybe his gut is all he has left.

He is coming round though. Gradually. His senses coming back to him. He's not dead yet. And if he's not dead he must be in some place.

He can see around him a little now, but just a little, the prison outside his head, and not only can he see but he can feel a little now too, he can feel the cold boards beneath his big body. Yes. That's it. Sensation! Sensation now. He's lying on the floor of a stage. Stage floor. Smooth, cool boards. This definitely has the contours of a stage. Has the feel of one. Been here many times before.

This place should feel like home, but it doesn't. It feels cold now, like an alien planet to which he has been abandoned – the crew have ejected him from their mission, he is cast aside, aghast, he will not last – just what part is he supposed to be playing here? Are there cameras filming? Is this being broadcast? To whom? For whom? By whom?

He hears no voices. No one is there to give him any instructions at all. No director. Who was that skinny man, long hair tied up at the back? No one tells him what to do. There is no script either. What is he to do ... just go ahead, make it up? He has never been good at making things up. *That's because you're an actor and it's not required of you. You're just paid to mouth what's already written down for you. No originality. If you've lived the life of a bored housewife you'd know that you have to be creative all the time.*

Lyd.

Millions of years.

Light years. Years of light.

Now only darkness. Caliginous. Where is she when he needs her?

I'd better go check on the turkey.

She is checking on the turkey, lest it escape from the oven. Yes, there had been a joke, a party, a Christmas party. Hats! Is this Christmas Eve? Or has all that gone past? Already a new year.

He only hears the deep thrumming of the blood inside his head, his own heartbeat, thudding there, insistent, blood flooding around him, persistent. He's not dead. He's got that much right. He's still here. But where?

In a theatre, yes, sure. Must be.

The lights of this place slowly rising, like the beginning of a play, illuminating a scene; yes it's a theatre he is in, but he does not know his lines, he has not rehearsed. He does not remember there being any rehearsals. When that happens one realises one is in a dream. Oh, he's been there before all right, years and years of such dreams, like the ones where you have no clothes on, or that you have not studied for the final maths test, or you haven't learned your lines, you haven't learned your lines, you haven't learned your lines. So, what are you going to say? But he is not in a dream. It feels too real to be a dream. The boards underneath him, solid and cold. The smell of the place, the wood and curtains and the smell of the fabric on the seats, of the audience and the perfumes they drag in with them, night after night, the cloying colognes, the fruity flavours, and the make-up, the plastering they have put on, and you too, the make-up you put on at the mirror, face paint, war paint, staring at your own face. Who are you? You are an actor. You play a role. Is it as simple as that? No, who are you *tonight*? Someone else. Always someone else, never playing the real you ... that would shock an audience to its core.

Bit by bit the place gets a little brighter. But it's still caliginous. It's still dim, dun, shadowy, obscure. He is trying to adjust his eyes. His eyes are old now, not quite what they used to be. His mind too, not quite what ...

Remarkable. He can recite lines of Shakespeare at length but can never remember to put the bins out.

What?

Who said that? Lyd! Lyd! The dustbins, Lyd!

Mr. Godot told me to tell you he won't come this evening but surely tomorrow.

And that! Who said *that*?

He remembers the scene, watching from the wings. A boy. Just a young lad.

Charles is not in the wings now. He is on the stage. It should feel like home.

It doesn't.

He pulls himself up to a seated position. He is on his bottom now. He is no longer lying down. A bit of strength comes back to him. He's not dead yet. He will get himself out of this mess. A momentary stress. He will figure it out. But his head hurts. Groggy. He's sluggish. He cannot seem to think straight. What does that even mean: think *straight*?

The lights go up, ever so slightly brighter, ever so slightly more, a minuscule improvement, his whereabouts, which theatre is this?

And there's a chair there. He's only just noticed it now. There's a chair, right in the middle of the stage. How did that get there? An empty chair. Like it is waiting for him. He crawls towards it. He gets there. He climbs upon it. He sits. What now? A light should come on. A big light. But no light comes on.

How come there is no one about? No audience. No cameras. No people of any description ... wait ...

There is.

He thinks he can hear the breath of someone out there in the audience. Out there in the dark. People. There must be people there watching him. People were always there watching him. That was his job. That was what he was paid for. Entertain. The spotlights. The TV cameras. The affection, yes, they had real affection for him. That was what he was paid for. He wanted them to like him, all of them, like him.

Shadowy figures, yes, out there, the front rows, yes, they must have paid good money; he can hear breathing, yes. His mind may be going, his memory, and his eyes, too, but not his ears, oh no, not yet: *I think the King is but a man, as I am ...*

Are those spectators? Who is looking at him? Who sees? This must be some piece of experimental theatre, that bloody claptrap, where they give you no script at all and lead you out into some scenario and you are to make it up as you go along. They might hand you some useless props, tell you to improvise, even the audience might participate, good God, who ever heard of such nonsense, audience participation! Is that what this is? Some rubbish like that? Some drama students' game? Postmodern piss. Oh grow up; he's a professional, one eminent critic once remarked ...

But he can hardly see anything.

His head hurts.

Can somebody see him?

Who's there?

Nay, answer me: stand, and unfold yourself.

He realizes that his hands are now free. They had been shackled but now they are free! This comes as some kind of revelation. His wrists are sore where the binds had chaffed him. He scratches at them but it brings no relief. His wrists are sore. His head is sore. What had they given him? What drug had knocked him out? Yes! He had been drugged. He had been drinking wine at home with his family, it had been Christmas Eve! Christmas bloody Eve! Is it still? Is it now? What day is it? What time is it? *Have you not done tormenting me with your accursed time!* Where is he? *'Tis bitter cold and he is sick at heart.* He knows who he is. He is Charles Cunningham. Actor, renowned of stage and screen ... but none of that matters now. All that matters now is to find out ...

Ben!

The lights of the theatre go ever so slightly brighter, ever so slightly hotter.

Ben!

That is the name of his son's boyfriend. Ben: that's who it was who brought him here. He remembers now.

And two big men. Two hulks. Like circus strongmen. Did he even see them? He had felt them, grappling him. They were enormous.

They had bundled him into a van. His eyes were closed but he felt the fall. A van, yes! He remembers that now too. He was brought here against his will! Against his will!

Kidnapped: is that what this is all about? His will. His money.

Aren't you going to read the instruction?

Instruction? There's no joke?

No, this is more of a…game kind of thing. That's the surprise! If you'll play along…

He had been looking at his Christmas tree. Fairy lights flickering. He had been talking with his wife, or had they been arguing? Sherry. Dustbins. Bach. Bublé. Lost notebooks. They often argue. The most trivial things. Or not even that, not even arguing, just bickering. About little things, about things that don't matter at all. Where is she now? Lydia. Where is his wife? And his son, David? Where is David now? Shouldn't he be with Ben?

Ben.

Ben.

The boyfriend. The dark, rangy, mysterious one. It had been their first meeting. It had been going rather well. They had laughed, and they had joked, and he had pulled a cracker, and he had put on a party hat, but after that…

What happened after that?

Wine.

They'd drunk some wine. Ben had opened the wine, deft with the corkscrew, muscly arms on him, pulled it out with a pop. He had poured it into glasses. They had all drunk from it. Had Ben drunk from it too?

At precisely six o'clock look out the living room window.

But it is Charles Cunningham here alone on the stage. He feels like he has been here before. The smell of this place. Every theatre kind of smells the same, but they all had their unique qualities too. Like good wine if you had a nose for it: you could catch hints of raspberry or strawberry or cinnamon. Maybe Charles had a good nose for different theatres. The large auditoriums, the quaint village halls, the new modern ones with their clever multimedia technology…

This is not a West End theatre, it feels smaller, feels newer. This is somewhere outside the city. In the suburbs. Or this is near to where he lives. Closer to the countryside. Provincial theatre. He thinks he's been here before. Has he?

The lights brighten further. He can see a tree now. There is a tree on the stage. He knows this tree. He has seen one very similar to it before. A long time ago. It might not be the original Giacometti one, but it looks very similar, it looks like a copy, everything looks like a copy of that Giacometti original one. Yes, this is the tree from *Waiting for Godot*. He knows this tree. He's been near this tree before, or near something very similar to it. Remembers ropes and bowler hats and a young boy who says his brother minds the sheep and his master doesn't beat him because he must be very fond of him.

Extraordinary the tricks that memory plays!

What's going on?

A crack of a whip then from out of nowhere. It cracks right in front of his chair, in front of his feet. It scares the life out of him; his heart skips a beat, or maybe more than a beat, several stuttering beats, as he tries to catch his breath, he's scared to almost-death.

A figure emerges from the side shadows, from the caliginous, from the wings, from the past, a whip-bearer, a man now. And this man stands in front of Charles Cunningham, armed and frightful, and he violently cracks his whip once more.

25

Janie and Patrick are looking at the contents of the cracker that have spilled out onto the pub table.

"Usual junk."

"Not this time," says Janie. "Look at this."

"What is it?"

"A message."

Janie is holding a piece of paper in her hands and is reading from tiny, printed writing. She has to hold it close to her face to make out all the words.

"Don't be alarmed, but your urgent assistance is required."

Patrick's interest is more than piqued; the pint he was going to order is forgotten.

She continues, *"Please go to this address and untie the two people you find bound to their dining-room chairs. These people have been drugged but are not in any way hurt, nor are they in any future danger. There is no need to call the police; doing so might only put the third (absent) person in danger."*

"What the fuck is all this about? Some kind of joke?"

"Joke?" says Janie. She hadn't even considered it; perhaps the wannabe criminal psychologist was taking over and she is enjoying the unexpected drama of the situation.

"It might be like one of those mystery games. Like those real-life Agatha Christie role-play parties they have in country houses. Where they have to guess the murderer and so on. It might be like that."

"Might be. But why involve us? What have we got to do with anything?"

"Maybe we were just convenient."

Janie considers.

"Those two at the pumps. The tall, broody guy with the dark eyes. I knew there was something odd about him."

"Ah, now, Nancy Drew..."

Whether Janie gets the reference to the super-sleuth or not, she gives no indication, something else has just crossed her mind.

"No, we weren't just convenient."

"What do you mean?"

"We were targeted. That's why the security cameras were smashed. So we wouldn't see their faces."

"But we can remember them, their faces."

"Can we? Would you be able to pick them out? Look around you. They could even be here right now, watching us."

They look around at the pissed-up carousing, the raucous revelling – some have clearly left their places of work, knowing this is the start of holiday season and are about to make the most of it. If the country is in political turmoil it certainly doesn't show at holiday times, people are well able to compartmentalise, priorities: booze first, the rest can wait till January.

She was right. Neither of them would be able to pick out the two from earlier that day. Their features blurred the more you thought about them – even though the tall one had had his face right up to hers. He was dark, good-looking, his hair closely cropped, but it could be the description of a dozen here.

"But why us?" says Patrick, happy now after a bellyful of booze to play a Hardy boy to her Nancy Drew.

"Because we're helpful. Ordinary, and helpful. And because it's not too far from here."

She points to the address written on the back of the paper.

"Those guys have thought it all out. Shit, I think I remember now!"

"Remember what?" asks Patrick.

"A few days ago, there was a black van parked across the street from the garage. A creepy guy, big, thuggish, was watching me, watching everything I did. I think he was even filming, on his phone. When I stared at him I must have spooked him because he put the phone down and drove away."

Patrick is looking at the address, "That's a posh area. What do you think is going on? Robbery?"

"Probably."

"Are we going to go?"

"You don't have to," she says. "He gave the cracker to me. It's my responsibility."

"Well, you're not going alone, that's for sure. I'll come with you."

He pauses to take a drink and to wonder if any of this is wise.

"You don't think we should tell the police?"

"No. Someone … the third person, whoever he or she is, might be put in danger, we can't risk it. Let's just go."

The whole thing has taken a rather surreal turn. Just a few hours ago they were filling cars and lorries with petrol and diesel, wiping windscreens, and wishing customers a Merry Christmas. Now they are embroiled in some adventure game that might be, as Patrick suggested, a joke, an elaborate hoax, or might also be very real, no gag at all, whatever the case may be they're on it, embroiled sure, embroiled.

They both pick up their drinks and down them in one go. Janie stuffs the cracker and other pieces into her bag.

They rise from the table and make their way through the bustling crowd, envying the frivolity of the masses, unsure of where the night will lead them.

26

"You," says Charles Cunningham, looking up and addressing the whip-bearer, eyes full of hurt and spite now that they have fully opened and adjusted to this most distressing situation.

"Me," says Ben Morrigan, leering down on the seated man. "Yes, it's me."

The lights, while not fully up on the house, are bright enough for them both to examine each other. They had sized one another up at the entrance to his grand house, they had sized each other up when they entered the dining room before the feast that had been laid out before them, but right here right now is the entrance to something else entirely, a portal to a whole other dimension; their eyes lock on one another, Ben refusing to blink – these are the eyes of a man taking charge.

Brick has left his lighting duties and has seated himself next to his brother in the front row of the otherwise empty audience. The twins sit back, relaxed, as if they are going to enjoy the spectacle, relish what will play out in front of them. They've never even seen a real play before; if this is to be a Christmas pantomime they realise there is no one to shout out *look behind you*, there is no one to offer any kind of assistance at all. But they are happy to sit on those plush seats in silence, and see what their instructor has set up for their amusement.

The man in the chair has never felt so alone in his life, weeping softly there, utterly scared – even the brothers can see the puddle of urine that has gathered at the old man's feet, his crotch stained and stinking, it's all part of the spectacle. Ben Morrigan doesn't seem to mind one bit, is in complete control of what unfolds: he is the playwright, the director, and now he is playing the part he has been rehearsing for years.

"Well, here we are, your natural environment. It's like bringing a gorilla back to its habitat. All so very heart-warming."

Brick and Brac both grunt out a laugh from their seats.

"Feel free to stand up and stretch your legs. It must have been cramped in the back of that van, and you all trussed up like a turkey. We never did get to finish all that meat did we?"

Ben keeps the whip tight in his grip.

"Go on, rise, this is your arena. You might not remember but you've been here before. I'm sure it'll come back to you. A different theatre, but the same set. An exact copy."

Charles gets off the chair. He looks down at his wet trousers but oddly feels no shame – too late for all that now, too late for everything. His eyes sting with tears, regretful, but no shame yet.

"It's a little cold in here; cold without an audience ... we're not allowed to put on the heating. We're not allowed to be here at all actually, not at this time of night. But I am working here again. Props. Set design. You'll remember that tree. I made it. Go on, look at it. Based on the one from years ago ... how many years ago now, doesn't matter, does it? Go on, take a closer look."

Charles looks at the tree, but he is not truly focused on it; he is wondering as to why he is here, what circumstances have landed him on this stage – yes the place does feel familiar, everything about it bringing a sense of déjà vu, perhaps deep down he has always known that this day would come.

"You've been examining trees all day," laughs Ben. "This one won't fall down though. Made of sturdier stuff."

Ben cracks the whip off the floor, startling the old man, startling even the big brothers in their comfortable seats.

"What is it from? That tree. Which play, I mean?"

"*Waiting for Godot*," says Charles, his voice small and broken.

"Well done," says Ben condescendingly, as if he is now talking to a very young child, or someone mired in senility.

"Do you remember that you starred in that play a long time ago? *Waiting for Godot*."

Charles looks crestfallen, he shakes his head.

"Oh, come on now, you can do better than that."

The actor plonks himself back on the chair again; he holds his head in his hands and gently tugs at his hair.

"Right. Let's start with something easier first. A little warm-up. You actors are used to that, warming up before the main event, and this could be a long night, we don't want to get it too taxing for you at the beginning. So, I'll tell you what. We'll do it like Estragon and Vladimir, the two characters from Godot. Very fast rapport. Answer as fast as you can now. Right?"

Charles doesn't lift his hands from his head until Ben cracks the whip once more and the brothers applaud the terrific terror of it.

"Up, pig!" Ben snaps, then manages a little laugh. "See, that was a line in the play, too. Remember that? It was your line actually. No ... nothing?"

Charles shakes his head again but he keeps his eyes on his tormentor.

"Right," says Ben. "Here we go. What's your name?"

"Charles Cunningham."

"Where are you from?"

"London."

"Where were you born?"

"Lewisham."

"What year?"

"1957."

"Yes, we all know that."

"What?"

"Never mind. What year is it now?"

He has to think.

"2019."

"Correct. You're doing just fine ... a few more. What's your wife's name?"

"Lydia."

Charles chokes with emotion on saying her name, wondering if he will ever get to see her again; a force of snot erupts from his nose, he wipes it away messily with his shirtsleeve.

"Maiden name?"

"Connell."

"Son's name."

Charles looks at him spitefully, "You know his name."

"Yes, I do. I do indeed. My lover. My lover. Little Davey boy. Poor thing. So lost. Likes a party. Not so good with the books – bright, but lazy."

Charles hangs his head and tugs at his hair once more.

"Where are you going tomorrow?"

"Tomorrow?"

"Yes, tomorrow, isn't there somewhere you are supposed to be?"

Charles looks alarmed but remembers, "Yes, yes, travelling."

"Where?"

"Greece."

"Very good. Your memory might not be so bad after all, short-term at least. Rumours of your cerebral demise have been greatly exaggerated."

"Demise?"

"Not yet, not yet, dear fellow," Ben intoning at his haughtiest, "but we might get there. Patience, a little patience is required, I've been waiting a long time to get all this right."

"Get what right?"

"This. This whole thing. My play. Some things take time. Careful planning. No point in rushing it now that we are here. Wouldn't you agree?"

"I've no idea what you are on about. I don't know what you want."

Ben sighs.

"All in good time."

Ben circles around the chair menacingly. Charles watches him, his knees now evidently trembling.

"You know, seeing you like this, befuddled and shaking there in your old-man clothes, your old-man skin, you might actually make a very good King Lear. If only you could remember your lines. See, that's the thing. In a play like Lear, there are just so many. And it's so easy to forget. Especially at your age. Or is it that we choose to forget some things and remember others? Is that it? Selective memory? Is that what they call it?"

Charles looks off into the distance, out past the audience of two to the exit doors at the back of the theatre.

"Oh, I wouldn't even think about making a run for it. Do you think you'd get past me?"

Ben points at his accomplices.

"Do you think you'd get past them?"

Ben's laugh echoes around the empty spaces of the hall and the twins join in, strengthening it.

"Great sound in here, don't you think? We're going to have a marvellous production. But then it is a great play, isn't it? All about waiting. And – spoiler alert – you now he doesn't come don't you? Godot? He never arrives. See, the waiting is everything. Our play here tonight is a little different because, there is waiting, sure, but there is a denouement. There is a climax and all gets revealed. Truth, if you like."

Wearily, Charles says, "I have no idea what you are babbling on about. Take me back to my wife and child or you'll end up behind bars."

Brick and Brac laugh like it is the funniest line they've heard in ages, as if they are witnessing a comedy and Charles is the fool of the piece – it was so much better than being stuck at home with Christmas telly.

"What do you want from me?"

"I want your final great performance. They won't cast you as King Lear. You're past it. Your frail state. You'd never make it. And after tonight's mental ... upheaval ... no, no Lear for you, but you can give us your last great performance here, now, look, you even have a captive audience."

Brick and Brac are smiling back and waving.

"Consider it like an improv session. I'll throw out a few scenarios or prompts and you improvise around them. How about that? You can say anything you like. Make it up if you want. Or tell the truth, doesn't matter a fuck really. Just get it out."

"Why?"

"Why not? We're both in the theatre business. And we both like to play, don't we?"

Charles hangs his head and sobs softly again. He knows where he is and yet he does not know where he is. Physically, yes, a theatre, a stage, but he does not know why he is really here, cannot see the reasons behind it. All he knows is that he is being held by these three people, and one of them the boyfriend of his only son. But that's it. What is *really* going on? He chokes up again when he thinks of his wife and son; they had been sleeping there, right at the dining table. Charles had held the knife aloft and brought it down on the flesh of the cooked bird. Carved it into slices. How he wishes he had it now, that knife, he could plunge it into the body of his captor, or turn it on himself, into his own fading heart.

"Well, do you not want to play along? This is your home. Right here. On the stage. The finest actor ... what was that quote again? Never mind. You were born to tread the boards, so, let's do it. I'll play my part too. We're in this together. You and me, what do you say?"

Brac lets out a wolf whistle.

"See, your fans are waiting. You're not going to let them down now, are you? You're not going to let me down, or your family? You're not going to let yourself down, are you? A man of your pride, your esteem! You've never let yourself down in the past... have you?"

Ben feigns aggrieved shock.

Brick and Brac applaud from their seats.

Charles rises, rises to his full length and tries to sticks out his chest. His knees buckle.

The twins applaud even louder now and Ben shouts to the rows and rows of empty seats:

"Ladies and gentleman, it looks like we have a play on our hands!"

27

J anie is driving an old 2006 Honda Civic LX, having never gotten around to updating to a newer model. Her father was as loyal to that particular car as he was loyal to his job at the Honda Company in Swindon that manufactured it. When Janie moved with her mother to Essex first and then London after his death, they swore they'd change it, or just sell it, and have no car at all, they could bus and Tube their way around, but Janie didn't have the heart, and here she is now pushing it to its 1.8-litre inline four-cylinder engine limit, and Patrick Fenton sits petrified in the passenger seat.

"Slow down for fuck's sake, you'll get us killed."

"We've got to make it in time. Make sure there's no one hurt."

Janie has imagined destruction all over a posh house. Bodies littered. Blood seeping into shag carpets. Satanic messages scribbled across mirrors. Occult symbols on the walls. She has imagined a house torn apart and emptied out by a team of expert thieves, and shaken, damaged victims tied to chairs, gagged and bruised, possibly even...

She is the type to let her imagination get the better of her and it is one of the reasons Patrick likes being with her – she made the grey garage days gallop; perhaps it was just a youthful thing, perhaps he had been that way himself a long time ago and lost it somewhere along the route. Whatever. What he desires mostly now is that she just slows the heck down or there'll be blood spatters all over this car too.

"Do you know the way?"

"It's written down."

The car is thirteen years old, no satnav, it's lucky to be allowed on the road at all, if they need to check the exact location, the locus of their current unexpected adventure, they'll just have to check their phones.

Not only is Patrick worried about the speed the car is travelling at, he is also worried about the prospect of cops appearing from behind some corner at any moment, blue lights flashing and making them pull over. He is worried about the whole endeavour, wondering whether it might have been a better idea to have stayed in that pub, or gone back home and behaved as normal folk do.

Janie notices the fret all over his face, "I can stop and let you out if you want."

"No. No. We've come this far."

"Right then ... hold tight."

She puts her foot even further to the floor.

They pull up in front of the big, black gates of the Cunningham residence. She switches off the engine and matches the address on the slip of paper with what she has summoned on her phone.

"I think this is it."

"Impressive."

"What? The house ... or my driving skills?"

He cannot believe that she is not shaking, cannot believe how controlled she is given the circumstances. Is it the adrenalin kicking in, or is she just not right in the head? Patrick always had his doubts about the younger generation, but perhaps those brought up on video games or Chessington amusement park rides were always going to gravitate towards greater thrills. He was from a more sedate era, where a packet of crisps and a can of Coke bought by a father was the extent of excitement, and besides the Saturday football results coming in at five o'clock, thrills were for people on TV.

They are not surprised to find the gates wide open, the team of thieves they have imagined must be well and truly out of sight now.

They drive right through the gates and through the grounds, winding their way down the driveway, Janie making the decision to do this without her headlights on and crawling forward at a snail's pace.

Patrick is quite certain that she has spent too many hours watching detective dramas on TV to have ideas like these come to her so effortlessly, but he has to admit, she seems to know what she is doing.

"Last chance to turn back," he says before they cross the threshold of the large house, but the withering, emasculating look she returns is enough to tell him never to be so timid in her presence again – he follows her right in.

They make their way tentatively through the hallway and are quickly enraptured by the lavish surroundings – no wonder this place is a target for thieves – the place is magnificent. The blank square spaces on the walls where paintings recently hung look oddly bereft, and the naked plinths and side tables silently decry their violation across the marmoreal floors.

Janie and Patrick hear moans and groggy groans and they make their way towards them, heartbeats rising with every step.

The sight presented in the dining room might not be the gorefest Janie had imagined, but it is a crime scene all right, and there's no backing out now: Lydia Cunningham and her son David, both bound tight to their chairs in front of a table rich with Christmas pickings, now have their eyes open and are registering the sight of the strangers with alacrity.

"Oh, thank God," gasps Lydia. "Cut off these ropes, please. I beg you."

"Are you the only two here?" asks Janie, warily.

"Yes," David yelps, "only us. Get us out of this fucking mess."

But Janie doesn't.

Not yet.

Because Janie needs time to consider.

Janie needs to take all this a little more slowly.

For all the mad-dash rushing around and getting here, she is now deciding on a different tack; she turns to her partner:

"Can we talk outside for a second?"

Patrick follows her out of the room to the anger and bewilderment of the tied-up two squirming behind.

In the hallway Janie paces, frowning with thought.

"What's wrong?" her partner asks.

Impassioned, desperate pleas come for the dining room but they are ignored.

"Let's just take a minute to browse around."

"Browse? What are you talking about?"

"They might not have taken everything."

Patrick cannot believe where he is; he should be at home with his family; he cannot believe that a half-hour ago they were both slurping on their drinks listening to that John Lennon song about some war being over – but here he is in a stranger's house with his workmate and he cannot believe what she is saying – the two people pleading for them to return may be in need of medical assistance, in need of an ambulance.

"Shut the fuck up!" Janie shouts back at the angry couple when they cry again, "we'll be there in a minute."

"Are you serious?" Patrick says.

"They're fine. There's nothing wrong with them. Let's just take a quick gander around, see if there's anything left over."

Patrick is incredulous. She had spoken about a possible career with the police, her dream of being a criminal psychologist or some kind of profiler, but here she has gone the opposite direction altogether – how quickly things get turned on their head.

"Left over? The police could be on their way right now!"

"Why would the police be on their way right now? They know fuck all about this. Let's just do this quickly."

Patrick follows her.

Patrick always follows her.

For a man more than twice her age, for a man who took her under his wing when she first started to work at the garage, he kowtows to her. Pathetic, really, for a man of his years, but he follows her up the stairs and into the master bedroom.

Janie immediately starts rifling through a jewellery box and begins stuffing rings and necklaces into her bag and every available pocket.

"You're stealing!"

"Yes, of course I'm fucking stealing. I've got bills to pay, and this is my reward for untying those two downstairs."

Patrick's cannot block out the pleas from downstairs.

"Don't be so precious. The robbers have already taken all the art, so let's just take what we can. I don't know how the thieves missed all this."

With a lost expression, pitiful eyes, and with complete sincerity, Patrick says:

"But it's Christmas."

"It sure is," Janie says, laughing. She opens the wardrobe, her eyes widening at the bounty before her. "Look at all this stuff. Could fetch a sweet quid or two."

Patrick notices an attractive, possibly bespoke suit hanging on the man's side of the wardrobe.

"Do you think that would fit?"

She gives him a smile, glad he's decided to climb on board – it didn't really take that much after all. It's not thievery she reminds herself. It's reward. Reward. That is how she is justifying it. Reward for the rescue. They will release those two downstairs, of course they will.

"Take it. You can try it on later."

Janie takes two scarves from Lydia's side; Hermès, the tag reads, and they haven't even been worn. Score.

"Here, wrap one of these around your face," she tells him, "so they won't remember us."

"But they've already seen us."

"Briefly. But we don't want to strengthen their memory now do we? They still look a bit groggy, c'mon, just do it!"

They wrap the scarves around their faces and continue pillaging. Patrick takes the sharp-looking suit, bundling it up under his arm. They rush downstairs and out the main entrance, opening the car and flinging their loot into the boot.

They dash back into the house, Janie loving every mad moment of it and Patrick's pulse begins to quicken with the rush of it too.

When they return to the dining room the still-bound couple is naturally livid.

"For fuck's sake," David shouts, "what are you doing? Untie us! Call the fucking police!"

Patrick takes the carving knife lying on the table, and begins to saw at his ropes.

"Who the fuck are you anyway?" says David.

"Who the fuck are you?" says Janie, not for one moment about to give way in the power play; cunts should be fucking grateful they've come here at all.

When Patrick cuts Lydia loose from her binds she stretches and rubs the redness on her wrists.

Janie takes the knife from Patrick – wants to give them the impression that she could be dangerous, that they'd better watch themselves.

"Are you with Ben?" Lydia asks.

"Who the fuck is Ben?" says Janie, frostily.

She points the knife at David and Lydia, and, to Patrick's astonishment, threatens them.

"Listen you two, we don't know who the fuck you are, but we got a tip to come here…from a Christmas cracker…"

The words sound ridiculous coming from her mouth, but David and Lydia don't show the least bit of surprise.

She continues:

"We came here to untie you. That's all we are doing. We were told to tell you not to call the police. That the third person, whoever that is, will be fine. That there's no need to worry."

"No need to worry?" gasps Lydia. "Look at what's going on! My husband has been kidnapped!"

Janie and Patrick look at each other, a piece of the puzzle falling into place, but she retains her knife-brandishing, maintains her unflappable comportment.

"We don't know any more than that. This is just what we've been told. You got that?"

Mother and son nod, unsure whether this woman is to be feared or not. They do not know who to trust. All they wanted was Charles back, and they hadn't the foggiest notion of how to go about it.

Janie and Patrick start to back out the door and the Cunninghams can do nothing but watch them depart. They feel empty, violated, useless. The only morsel of sense they have gleaned from all of this came from the absurd word "cracker". What kind of twisted game is this?

Lydia goes to the bottle of wine that has sat breathing in the dining room. She holds it to her lips and greedily drinks from it. But as soon as she has taken a mere mouthful or two she begins to retch violently, spewing all over the dining-room table and right onto the bowl of Brussels sprouts that have sat withering and drying, pathetic little balls that no one wanted in the first place.

It is a joke, the whole thing, David thinks, watching his mother crumple into herself on the carpet.

Lydia has seen dramas like this: weeping stage mothers who have lost their families to war, or rape victims, torn apart physically and mentally by unknown perpetrators – Charles has even acted in some of those woeful plays. But this. This! This all happened right in her own house! She has not been raped, she has not really been physically harmed, but violated sure, and it is the house that has been raped. Her husband is missing. This is the worst thing of all. At least if the three of them were together they could try to work out who that Ben was, and what it was he wanted. But there is still too much mystery. She crouches foetal on the floor and her son can only look down upon her, both of them flummoxed. He is as lost as she is. He is as torn apart and sick with grief as she is.

He doesn't know how to comfort her. He is far too angry. Each breath he takes he swears at his own stupidity: how could he have been so...

But how could anyone have known? He had been with that man for months and months and...

What is it all about, this...saga?

What is the reason for all this?

Money?

Is that at the root of it?

David will walk the house and see what has been taken. He will check every room and take stock.

But he will not call the police.

He continues watching his mother cry and he tries not to give in to tears himself. He is trying to keep his composure, to not lose the run of himself, even though he has never been in an occasion quite like this – who has?

He takes deep breaths as he tries to steady his heartbeat, tries to release the clench of his buttocks, release the fingers that have balled up into tight fists, but the sound of a car outside vrooming down their own driveway interrupts such calming breaths and does nothing but push bile further up his throat.

Janie and Patrick are gone.

And David seethes.

28

The essence of drama: suspense. You buy your ticket and you have no idea where the story will go. Unless of course it is a well-known play. If it is *The Caretaker* or *Waiting for Godot* then everybody knows exactly what will happen. Or in Godot's case what will happen twice. It is down to the actors then to give performances with nuance, luring us into something we haven't witnessed before. But what is happening now on this stage is a complete mystery. It has not yet been written. This thing could go anywhere.

Ben walks to the centre of the stage. Charles pushes his chair to one side and plumps down upon it. He watches Ben, anxious but avid. He is as much spectator as participant. He is as curious as Brick and Brac are, on the edge of their seats. Nobody knows how this will fare, how it might end, how it might dare.

Charles may have found himself in one of those awful productions that are improvised on the spot, written on the fly, the kind of thing he has always detested, and there is nothing he can do about it. He has already been told that he cannot run away. He knows he is a prisoner to these people, a bind he has never been in before. Usually he is most free on stage, knowing what he has to do and rising to the occasion – *you're just paid to mouth what's already*

written down for you. No originality. But here, even with no
audience before him – save for two fearsome thugs – he has
never been so nervous. He has no idea what will happen, no
idea what this man Ben will say, what he will do. He has no
idea who Ben even is. And when it is his turn to speak, to
act, what kind of words will emerge? What will his creaking
old body decide to do? Will it surrender completely? Black
out? Will he fall down? Completely capitulate? The stain on
his crotch is cold, uncomfortable, not drying fast enough,
and he feels foolish and afraid. His knees have not stopped
quivering from the moment he woke up in the back of that
horrid van. He does not know where his wife and son are,
or whether he will ever see them again. On this stage he
realises he knows very little at all. He knows nothing of
this world and its hidden workings. He has never seen the
underbelly. He has lived in a bubble for years. Never been
truly challenged. Never threatened. He has been allowed
to forget, to live and forget. He has been worrying about
a Christmas tree all morning and whether it was standing
straight or not, or whether it would fall – this is the kind of
thing that has preoccupied him.

Ben looks out to the empty seats.
Ben has rehearsed some.
Ben tells.
He tells a story about two tall boys with tightly-cropped
hair playing hurling. He explains to the empty audience
that hurling is a Gaelic traditional sport, from Ireland –
where he has never been and has no intention of ever
going – that involves hard ash sticks and an even harder
small solid ball called a *sliotar*. This game was introduced to
the boys of a certain home by Irish nuns who cared for the

boys. They were told that it would make *men out of them*, that they were *unfortunate bastards* and would probably *never amount to anything*. They would even wield the sticks themselves, those short quick vindictive women in their hoods and capes – he did not know the names for such garments then – and they knew how much damage they could inflict, they could smash the very shins of Hercules, and were not humble about declaring it, or doing a little demonstration.

Ben mimes the swing of a hurley (the hurling stick) on this stage. He mimes catching a ball high in the air. He tells the empty audience that he played football too, the proper English one as well as the rougher Irish version, and rugby, rougher still, and all sort of sports, didn't matter which, but the Irish nuns – and the majority of them happened to be Irish for reasons he was, and remains, unsure of – preferred the *clash of the ash* as they called it, and enforced the sport on the boys, taught them how to hold those sticks high, taught them how to bruise and take bruises. It probably wasn't all that difficult to hand over hard sticks to young boys and tell them to beat the shite out of each other to their heart's content – what young boy was going to resist? The nuns used to say *shite*. Not *shit*. As if the extra *e* softened it, for the ears of the Lord were always listening in. They said *feck* too instead of *fuck*. The children whispered them all.

The two taller boys had no trouble in wielding such sticks. And neither did the shorter boy who hung around with them, always in the middle – there was a perfect balance to that triumvirate: the two tall ones sandwiching the shorter one, and they went everywhere together. *Mates*: you needed those growing up, two were more than enough. Everywhere they would go, they would go together. There was a story once told to them – Sister Rose claimed it was Chinese in origin – about a man showing his sons how easy it was to break a single arrow. But add another to it and they became more difficult to snap. And try breaking three arrows tied tight together, damn near impossible. The boys remembered.

Charles watches.

Charles listens.

He does not know what any of this is about.

He does not know where this is headed, how this story will end. He had heard David talk about Ben's past, but David had skimmed over the details because he did not know himself.

Ben what?

What was his surname even? He had no idea.

Ben who?

Ben … what for?

What did any person know of another? What kind of secrets did each keep locked inside? So his wife booked a holiday to Greece without him knowing; so he went to the supermarket and bought wine and marshmallows, a whim – but surely there were worse things than those. This story of Ben is being presented with more detail, more colour, it is richer, and David probably knows none of this – where is his very own boy? His only son and heir. Is he still at home? And will the family ever …?

Charles hardly breathes, he takes in every word. Ben's words. A stranger's story.

And if his breath should stop completely …

That would be all right too.

If breath should stop …

And the curtain drop...

Then fine.

There is no way out of this.

He will have to face more of Ben's story.

He looks at the Godot tree. He remembers it. But nothing more than that. What part did he play?

Pozzo.

Pozzo.

Yes, that was it. But there was more to it than that. There was more that happened. Those times. He's sure of it. Those days. Gambolling. Younger, wilder days. Days of secret savagery. They just do not come to him, the particulars.

In drama school he learned how to read the lines, memorize them. Pretend to be other people. But who is he, and what did he do?

He watches Ben.

He listens.

Where is all this going now?

How does this story end?

Ben describes the shorter darker boy as having long, girlish hair and dark eyes. Ben rubs his own bristly head as he narrates. Perhaps no one will ever touch his head again. This does not matter. This does not really matter. Affection not Ben's thing. Never had the chance. Only ever allowed it in for...subterfuge.

He is an actor too. Ben is an actor too – Charles gets this now.

And what a performance!

He tells of the *sliotar* being belted around from boy to boy and the joy of the three of them together on those long summer evenings when evenings were elastic and stretched and stretched until someone came to pull you back indoors;

long days, idylls of the boy kings, and being motherless and fatherless didn't seem all that bad, there was freedom, as long as they had each other, the trio, and looked out for each other, the trio, as long as they had each other's backs.

They got bruised.

They made bruises in return.

Always those three.

Three together.

Trio.

Two tall skinhead ones.

One shorter, long-haired, girlish boy, with deep wells for eyes.

Triumvirate.

There were other kids, of course, but these three held tight, held tough, and the trio could not be broken.

And there was a dog.

This is what he is getting at now. Ben's tale. Ben's drama. This is where it is heading: there was a dog.

Ben talks about this big Rottweiler and Ben even barks to the empty audience in imitation of the beast. All these years later and he remembers its deep bark; it was forever at it, non-stop on those hot stretchy days of sunburn and sweat and mud-caked knees and pollen and midges, it was the sound of a volcano rumbling and readying to open, readying to empty its hot contents out into the world, that was its bark. Morning till dark.

It seemed it would never stop.

And it slavered.

Flapping jowls.

It was a horrendous thing that the nuns knew how to control but the kids did not, they stayed well clear – the kids for all their ill manners, ill tempers, ill origins, had nous enough to give the beast a wide berth – they were not the *eejits* their guardians often smote.

It barked.

The dog barked.

God but the fucking thing could bark. Morn until dark. Complaining of its chain. Complaining of life's pain. Complaining of the heat, of the thick black coat it was trapped inside.

Brutus.

That was its name.

Brutus.

The great betrayer.

And it felt entirely apt. It was *brutish*; it could do something *brutal* if it got free of its chain; it was a beast of *brute* force: Brutus. It could really have had no other name.

One of the tall boys, Richard, or was it James, picks up the *sliotar* deftly with his stick and sends it high into the sultry air and the long-haired lad has no trouble catching it on the end of his stick and playing it back again. Ben mimes all this. Ben is jumping wildly on the stage and Brick and Brac are practically bouncing on the edge of their seats with the excitement of this now, with remembrance. This all *then*, but this too: *now*. Redux. They have not seen him like this for a long, long time, not since those high-octane days, those days of running, sprinting; colts they were, young colts, hardly human at all, young muscles on the move, unstoppable: the way he speaks now, the way he narrates, and the images he conjures, casts a quick and witchy spell over the tittering two; they are there alongside him, those days, coltish days, alongside him, gambolling too, the trio. Usually this man is subdued, no teller of tales this man on the stage, a world of planning ever being meted out in his head, but here, a different story, a different story entirely, animated, come from behind the set for once, right out in front of it now, in front of this ghostly tree and ... *acting*?

Is this what acting is?

Is this *play*?

Or is this just recounting?

How can it be acting if what he says is the truth?

Charles Cunningham watches on, none the wiser.

Again, James – or is it Richard? – picks up the *sliotar* with his stick and sends it even higher into the air this time, testing his mate, and the shorter lad has no trouble catching it on the end of his stick and playing it back again even as his locks spill into his eyes. This could go on all day. This could go on all the livelong day. The back and forth of it, through dandelion puffs and swarms of midges and nectar-carrying bees, through the beams of the sun until they wane and become weary of the day, until then, back and forth, the easy repetition, the *puck* and *pock* sounds, this could go on hour after hour until their arms grow weak from overexertion or they can no longer see the little white ball in the gloaming.

But it doesn't.

It doesn't go on at all.

For it stops abruptly.

All of a sudden.

Because the boys have become distracted.

A young married couple is coming out of the orphanage door and they are talking with one of the nuns, Sister Bernadette, or Sister Rose, it is hard to make out which it is from where they are with the sun and the perspiration trickling into their eyes.

The couple is a married couple. That much is clear. Newly. Palpable. It's in the way they cling close to one another. The way she leans on him as he leads, with longer strides and she struggles to keep up – he seems keener to get out of the grounds than she does, looks like he wants on his way. The boys and girls know that this is usually the case, the women linger longer, they have more hurt in their eyes, some pain still manifest, some loss never accepted – *I'm afraid you are unable to conceive* – the children know this and they try to exploit it, even the little children know, innately: take *me*, love *me*, I am the best you could ever hope for.

The three adults talk as they walk and the boys are transfixed. So too are all the other satellite children that orbit the scene, eyes on stalks, ears pricked up and trying to pick up a scrap of dialogue. They all want to know the outcome of this. They all have a chance. It is an equal playing field. *All children are equal in the eyes of the Lord.* This is what the nuns reiterate. Equal. But how true is it? Some are older than others. Some are cuter and better behaved than others. Some are sicker, more depraved. Some are thieving, others slaves. It is not at all a level playing field. It is a field full of bumps. There is nothing level about it. All children may be equal in the eyes of the Lord but not in the eyes of a young, married couple who has had a world of trouble and are here to consider others, consider options, alternatives.

The boys have their desperate eyes on them.

The couple walks towards the car with the nun.

The children know they are not allowed to approach. Whatever transaction has been done ... has been done. It is all over. Decisions made.

The man opens the door for the woman. She brings a handkerchief to her eye as she sits herself in.

The man shakes the nun's hand. It is all very business-like.

He shakes his head. He has probably done this already, but he does it again. There is nothing that the nun can do to change his mind. She can see that. Over. Done. Everyone can see that. No one here is good enough.

The nun – it is Sister Rose, they realise now, having wiped the sweat and focused – taps the man on the shoulder. Is that tap a consolation? Or is it understanding? *I can't blame you, sir.*

At the end of the day it all means *no.*

Simple as that.

No means no.

Not this time.

Sorry.

Perhaps not ever.

And the dog?

The dog just keeps on madly barking. The canine is completely insane. Although the scene seems like it has been carried out in breathless silence, it has not been that way at all, for the dog has barked and grumbled all the way through it, looking for water in its bowl, looking for release, looking for the Devil to rise up from the scorching depths and take him by the lead, anywhere, anywhere, but away from this scorching spot.

The car drives off.

The shorter boy places the *sliotar* on the end of the hurley stick. He balances it there, expertly. He bounces it, jiggles it, then lets the ball jump up a yard or two into the air and with a big arching swing pucks the *sliotar* right through the summer air with a deadly aim.

The ball lands directly in the open mouth of the barking dog. It sticks right in there, jammed.

The dog begins to choke, gasping to fill its lungs, and it collapses on the dusty ground, its chain forming a noose now only tighter around its neck.

The nun comes running across the grounds, yelping frantically, her garments spread like a running vulture, fast as her sixty-year-old feet will take her.

The twins are smiling, grinning from ear to ear.

No more barking, they are thinking, no more of that.

Peace, be still. These words read from the Bible to them only the day before. Mark 4:39.

The long-haired boy leans on his stick, wipes the sweat from his brow. Job well done. He looks at the two he is sandwiched between and he nods at them. Then all three drop their hurling sticks at their feet and move to a shaded area, where the building casts a heavy shadow.

The dog writhes. The nun desperately tries to free the ball from the mouth of the beast but she is having no luck, it is jammed in there tight, and the stupid animal has only clamped down more upon it, its yellowy back teeth sinking deeper.

Does it not know how to breathe through its nose, the stupid mutt? Does it not even know how to save itself?

Perhaps it does not matter, because the chain is now wrapped around its neck lessening any chance of air reaching its lungs. It has no chance.

The feverish, fervent children all watch with excitement. There is an air of immense delight about them, but they cannot release it – they must keep it under wraps, keep it trapped, they have to appear horrified, the poor dog, poor Brutus. They must act like they care.

The nun gives up. She sits back on her haunches, letting the beast take its final quivering breaths. Then she rises with rage and heads towards the three idling boys.

They stand still.

They wait for her little legs to reach them in the cool shade, flying they must be, underneath the black covering, little legs going like the clappers.

The boys face her down.

"Which one of you yobbos was it? Tell me now."

They say nothing. Not the chattiest blokes in the world on the best of days, they certainly won't be drawn into conversation right now.

Their eyes are cold, frigid faces bold.

They reveal nothing. Zilch. They do not budge. They do not twitch. They hardly blink.

"All three of you then. You'll regret this. Into the office now, all three of you, go, go!"

Sister Rose knows it is useless to tackle them here, what with their audience of admirers looking on. She turns away from them, spitting curses to the heavens as she goes, scattering children like sparrows – the little ones flee to hedgerows, they hide behind walls.

The three boys turn slowly and they follow the dusty path she kicks up. But they are not in any rush. They are not frantic like she is. They are not flustered. They had a job to do, a problem to solve and they did it. They are lackadaisical in their walk. They've got all the time in their world.

They hear nothing now, no barking, no noise at all. And if they listen really closely they can just catch the sound of the married couple's car motoring off into the distance. Another chance gone. Just another.

The kids all skip back into their play even more hysterical than before now, their bellies tremulous with the afternoon that's been – whether it will invade their dreams remains to be seen.

Charles listens to this story open-mouthed, just a gaping animal himself. But he has been riveted by it, like the children, and equally bamboozled as to the point of it all. Ben killed a dog. So what? Is it to say that he is capable of killing again, and has no trouble escalating from dog to man? Or is he saying that certain wrongs must be righted, that if you break the serenity of a summer afternoon you will be sure to receive your retribution?

The two in the front row applaud wildly, whistling their approval. This is the first real stage show they've ever seen; no one ever took their hands and led them to the theatre, not even for a Christmas pantomime. Surely this will never be topped. Is this what great drama is all about? Is this the thing? If it is always to be this entertaining they could find themselves coming again.

29

*T*hieves.

They can now be called *thieves*.

Or outlaws.

Bandits.

Robbers.

Janie's pockets are filled with gold and silver chains, necklaces, earrings, pearls too, classy stuff, and a classy suit is thrown in the back of the getaway car, waiting for Patrick's limbs to slip through.

They are rescuers too of course, heroes, this oddest of couples. They had cut the ropes of the prisoners and freed them … in their own house. What a bizarre few hours it has been since they pulled that Christmas cracker; how hard it is to even set it straight in their heads.

They know this much: it is Christmas Eve, it is raining in Ruislip, and they are very tired. They have exhausted themselves in the feat. Their hearts had pounded and have only quietened now that they are here, outside the Fentons' semi-detached house, breathing regularly, looking at the pink and green fairy lights flickering inside the windows. Patrick's mother had always kept an electric candle lighting in the upstairs window of their old house, his childhood home in Kilburn. Patrick has carried on the tradition and looks up at his own white candle lighting there now: it is meant to welcome the weary, it is supposed to say that anyone is welcome inside, no matter how downtrodden and hungry you are, you can find shelter under this friendly roof; it is a lovely tradition, and one he will strive to continue, it doesn't take much. He hopes his children will continue it too, when their turn comes around. The world needs such symbols. Lights to guide. To make your fellow man feel safe and not remind of the failings and fragilities of humanity, the sense of doom that ever looms.

They sit in the car while the radio plays yet another tacky Christmas song. They are old already, all these songs, heard only once a year but so very very old, tiresome.

Janie turns the radio off.

Patrick take his eyes from the candle in the window and looks at his partner-in-crime.

"What have we done?" he says, and to reiterate his lostness, his genuine crisis, he asks it again, "what have we done?"

Janie needs a moment to consider. There are so many ways his question could be answered. She could talk of it like it had been a mighty adventure they embarked on, in which they freed the captives, were successful; that they were actually heroes, really, heroes. Or she could admit that they had debased themselves entirely, that they were nothing more than lowdown thieves, as scummy as the faceless ones that got away with all the good stuff, the real hoard.

She opts for neither. A half joke instead, "We got our Christmas bonuses."

Patrick snorts.

What can he say to that?

There's no point in going over it all. It's already done. Too late to go back.

Maybe they would someday, when the dust had settled, years and years of candles later, tell a story to their grandkids perhaps, when Patrick has a white beard as long as Father Christmas, and a big belly to match, about their manic night, one chaotic Christmas Eve...would the grandchildren even believe it? *You've had one too many, Grampa, time for you to go to bed.*

"You'd better get inside," Janie says to him. "Big day for the kids tomorrow. Santa Claus is on his way. And don't forget your new suit."

Patrick reaches back, takes the stolen suit and folds it up neatly in his lap. He'll have to smuggle it in – that's another one he'll have to add to his list of outlaw roles, *smuggler* too.

All these years he thought he was just a regular bloke who liked his pint, worked in a service station, loved his wife and kids: a simple sort of bloke. All these years. Too late now. One chaotic night. Done. Do we know who we are? When that cracker gets pulled and instructions fly out...one should hope they are just stupid jokes, *knock knock*...

He leans over in the car and kisses his workmate on the cheek.

"Happy Christmas," he says, fondly. He means it. He wants her to be happy.

"Same to you."

"I'll see you at work in a few days."

"You will," she says, and she means it. She'll be there. He'll be there. The world keeps turning.

Patrick closes the door and heads towards the warmth of his house. He's got a lot of explaining to do. Or a lot of lying. To the woman sitting up in front of the telly, brandy in hand, wondering about him. *Where have you been?*

Patrick Fenton stops at his front door and turns. He sees Janie's car drive away into the rain-soaked distance. What has happened this night all feels slightly unreal, he's not even sure it all happened the way it did, was it just that Janie put a spin on it and that swept him up – how could he ever say no to such a woman? If he were twenty years younger he'd be head over heels in love with her for sure. Of course he would. Every man nearing fifty knows what he would be doing if he were nearing thirty. Every middle-aged man has that fantasy, that sense of regret too, that sorrowful ache that sits in the gut, knowing that life has somehow slid past without you being aware.

He is content enough though, turning the key in the lock, because he is returning to his family. He is returning to the people he loves and who in return love him completely. He is not in love with Janie Wilson, his effervescent workmate, he is just in awe.

And he's got a new suit under his arm. Reward.

30

"Right, get up, give me the chair. Let's just say this scene is in a house. A well-to-do house. Like your own."

Ben laughs.

Charles does not, but he obeys. He gets off the chair and sits on the cold, bare stage floor again. He wants no more of this. He has had quite enough, wants out. He's been subjected to so much: the drugging, the manhandling; he'd been thrown into the back of a van like a slab of butcher's meat, and that story... that story about the bloody dog, choking and dying in the hot sun... what do they want from him? What do these people want from him?

The only thing that comes to Charles is a horrible American phrase: *enough already*. Only that. A plea. *Enough already*. He must have heard it in some American drama. The only phrase that comes to him and it feels almost like a betrayal – he cannot think of anything better to say, nothing English and refined, nothing stage-worthy, he has no script in front of him.

Ben calls for the day's newspaper, the same one they perused in the morning, and Brac delivers it to him.

The twins remain agog. Front row. Best seats in the house.

Ben situates himself on the wooden chair, making out like it is the height of luxury. This acting lark. He crosses his legs and opens the tabloid newspaper. He starts tutting loudly, exaggeratedly.

A moment of silence descends before he starts tutting again, even louder this time, drawing laughs from the watching twins.

"Awful business really, don't you think so, darling?"

Ben looks at Charles on the floor. He whispers: *you're meant to be my wife in this scene,* loud enough for the twins to hear, and they respond with giggles again.

Charles, looking deathly pale, says nothing at all. *Enough,* he is thinking. Enough already. Enough of this charade.

"A wretched business, those movie stars and moguls and the wicked things they get up to, cavorting around, oh, it's just all so dreadful. Abuse of power, that's what I'd call it. An abuse of power."

Ben's inflections deliberately mimic those of a class above him. These are not orphanage inflections. Instead silver spoon susurrus. Not the rasp of the rotten.

Ben stage-whispers again, "It's like we're in a Pinter play ... just play along ... play, play, just play along."

Charles hangs his head. He is broken. Play? Play along? He cannot even speak. Enough already.

Ben bobs his head along the lines of the newspaper.

"Dear, oh dear. Another TV actor in trouble. Says here he was involved in an organised ring. My, oh my. A ring of 'em. Dear oh dear. How pernicious. This wanton world we live in. *As flies to wanton boys are we to the gods, they kill us for their sport.*"

Ben lowers the paper, glares at his *wife.*

"Know that line? It's from Lear. *King Lear.* Yes, yes, thought you might know it. *As flies to wanton boys are we to the gods, they kill us for their sport.*"

He keeps his eyes on him, on *her,* on his sullen, sulking wife.

"You are very quiet today, darling. Is everything all right? Is it the Christmas dinner? Is that what you are worried about? The turkey? I am sure it will all turn out just fine. Brussels sprouts and all. The boys will be here soon. Splendid."

Ben pauses.

"The two faggots."

He lets the line resound around the empty auditorium. The twins let out a laugh, what comedy they are witnessing! What talent on display!

"David and his lover. His lover! Ben! Wasn't that his name? Ben? Ben something. Ben what? Who knows?"

Ben gets up from his chair and stretches. He puts his hands behind his back and strolls casually around the stage as if he is in a garden now and admiring the topiary. He mimes picking up shears and pruning hedges. Where has all this acting talent come from? The quiet, brooding one. Or was *that* the act?

"Quite astonishing really, the crimes committed these days. Man's inhumanity to man. That's an old cliché that gets bandied about, eh? *Man's inhumanity to man.* I say, dreadful business altogether, what?"

Ben cannot stop himself from laughing now, corpsing right there in his own creation, and the twins naturally crack up along with him.

Such farce.

Ben steadies himself and continues with his creation.

"I really am quite disappointed in you, my dear. I thought since it was just the two of us here, we'd have a whale of a time. A whale! Dancing cheek to cheek on lovely moonlight evenings …"

Ben flings the imaginary shears away and waltzes across the stage with an invisible partner.

"… telling of our dreams and our ambitions. Our pasts, our worries, our secrets!"

Ben stops in his dancing tracks.

"What about those, eh? Secrets? Do you have any of those, darling? Anything coming back to you yet? I was sure that tree would spark it off. Some remnant … of something. Look at it."

Charles looks at the tree.

"Not very attractive, is it?" says Ben. "But it's not meant to be. It's meant to be almost dead. Lifeless. Certainly no Christmas tree. No fairy lights, ha! Fairy lights! Wherever did they get the name?"

Ben turns towards the audience and does a preposterous dance, "Look boys, look at me! I'm the Christmas fairy!"

The brothers explode in great roars of laughter but Ben gives them no time to settle to it. He rushes back to Charles and makes like he will kick him, drawing his leg back like a football player ready to volley home a screamer from thirty yards … but … he stops, his leg frozen in mid-air.

The twins, they watch Ben, motionless there, like a statue of a great player outside a stadium, frozen, bronzed. This drama! It's stupendous! They want Ben to follow through with this kick: *go on, go on, go on my son, kick 'im right in his fat, privileged face.*

But Ben doesn't. He stays frozen for a few moments longer and then he drops his leg.

He sighs.

He decides to go back to playing the husband in his warped drama. What is it? Kitchen sink or lounge-room nightmare?

"Still nothing, darling. That memory of yours. Not what it was, eh? They say we are able to lock away our traumas you know, we can box them up, throw away the key. There's probably a term for that, some psychological term. You see it with soldiers, PTSD, back from Afghanistan or some godforsaken place, having seen the most terrible atrocities, and they never talk about them. They just bottle everything up. It must eat you from the inside though, eh? Gnaw away at your old bones. Mustn't it?"

Charles shrugs.

"I said ... *mustn't it?*"

Charles Cunningham keeps his head down, says nothing. Enough. Enough.

"You know, I really think I'm losing the crowd here."

Ben looks out again to his captive audience of two.

"Ladies and gentlemen, you do know what we do with pantomime villains, don't you?"

The twins nod enthusiastically, delighting in the nonsense, knowing at any moment it could take a turn towards the macabre.

"That's right. We kick the living shit out of them. Would you like to see that girls and boys? Would you like to see someone get the living shit kicked out of them?"

The twins clap. Brick puts his fingers in his mouth and whistles. A wolf-whistle.

Wolf.

Big.

Bad.

It's turning into a fairy tale now.

What have we here? Have we been here before? *He's right behind you!*

"Imagine it's not what you see. Not even a Christmas tree. Imagine it's a beanstalk. How about that?"

Charles looks at him: now what? What now? Where to now? Enough.

"Yes, it's a beanstalk and Jack climbs up to the top, and do you know what he sees when he climbs to the top? A giant. Yes, you see, the giant is much bigger than the boy. Of course he is. He's a giant! He's meant to be. Everybody knows him. He gets everything he wants. And who's going to argue with a giant? No one. They turn blind eyes. Eyes blind. They turn. But the little one, Jack, he's just a skinny little thing in tights. Look at his skinny little legs. His no-rump. And his little bump in front. Tiny."

Ben sits right next to Charles on the stage floor. He stretches out his legs.

"Look, just skinny little legs. They're never going to be fast enough to escape the clutches of a colossus. Are they?"

Silence.

"Are they?"

Silence.

Ben springs up to a standing position. He looks down on the terrified actor trembling there. Ben's eyes are wide and flaming with derision. He looks like he could take chunks off him with his teeth. Chunks of his face with his very own teeth, an ear off maybe. He pulls his head back and speaks, his voice booming.

"But giants fall. They tumble in the end. They fall. That's how fairy tales work. Didn't you know?"

He looks out to the empty rows of seats, "You know, boys and girls, don't you?"

Ben walks right to the edge of the stage. He motions for the twins to come and join him. They oblige, naturally, darting and leaping up onto the boards, their muscles glad to be moving again, all that stasis has done them no good at all, they are men of action.

Ben shouts to the empty auditorium:

"And now, Ladies and Gentleman, the time of the evening has finally come, the moment you have all been waiting for. We present to you, one of the finest actors ever to grace the boards of London, or any stage anywhere. For the very last time on stage, naked, and unafraid, the final performance of the inimitable, Mr. Charles Cunningham!"

They strip him.

The twins tear every inch of clothing from him, rapidly roughly ravaging. They leave him standing there, without a stitch. He does not have the strength to fight them of course. Too soft to fight back.

Brac goes to the side of the stage and flicks a switch. A spotlight comes on. One solitary light, beaming down.

The light is directly on Charles Cunningham, bare and vulnerable, in the centre of the kind of stage he used to own.

In his head he had been screaming, *enough, enough,* but clearly that wasn't heard, that wasn't enough at all.

They want more. These are barbarians. They only want more. What kind of man is it that only wants more?

Ben and the brothers take their seats in the front row. They stretch out their legs and fold their arms.

The final scene is about to begin.

31

She pours herself two large Baileys. Her mother says she doesn't want ice so Janie doesn't bother putting any ice into either of the glasses. Janie doesn't care what she drinks now, as long as it has alcohol in it. As long as it hits that sweet spot. She'd been sitting with a ginger ale watching Patrick drink his pint and every other pisshead in the pub getting loaded up on a variety of cocktails, so she deserves this one. She hands her mother the glass and her mother sips from that, a soft Happy Christmas coming from her lips, barely reaching her daughter's ears.

There are twelve days of Christmas, traditionally. Janie wonders how many of these she's going to have to sit with her mother and hold her hand. Her mother has her good days. Mother can get around some evenings better than others. But those other days – Janie's not even sure her hips bother her all that much, thinks it's mostly in the head. The doctors don't disagree. Since her husband died that's mostly been the problem, and no pill has sorted it out yet. Sheila refuses any kind of therapy, any counselling. She says she just wants to spend time with her daughter, the only one who stayed home (Lisa upped and moved to Melbourne, Trisha to New York. Janie got left with a mop and a bucket: forget any fancy notions of catching criminals and going to lectures on profiling and the latest FBI technology being considered by Interpol and British intelligence, just clear that mess up).

Janie's drink is gone before she knows it. She pours another. Her mother has barely touched hers and stares at the Christmas cards on the mantelpiece. Reindeer. Snow. Robins. Baby in a manger.

Of course Janie is now a criminal. She stole from that house, which makes her dreams of being involved in police work all the more risible. She did do something vaguely heroic, cutting free the flabby little son – it had been that curly bloke from the petrol pump; she realized that after, and his uppity mother. And she realized too that the darker one must've been the brains behind the operation. So, if she really had crime-fighting in her veins – Patrick called her Nancy Drew, who the hell was Nancy Drew? – then what she should do is call the police and tell them all that happened. But Janie has got jewellery spilling out of her pockets, so it's far more likely that it is criminal blood that flows through her – maybe she could look into her family tree, find out where she really comes from. Who are we anyway? Who are we?

Janie pours another glass. Her mother has fallen asleep in her favourite chair.

Janie will pour petrol for another few months at that service station.

Janie will try and sell the jewellery, though she doesn't quite know how to go about doing that.

Janie will never work for the police. She might take a week in New York with her sister, but that will be the longest she will ever leave her mother.

Janie will figure it all out eventually. She will.

All she knows right now – on her third glass of Baileys – is that she has just had the best day in years. Nothing has come close to the putting of foot to the floor in her dad's old car, the speeding through quiet Christmas streets, the trespassing on another's property and the stealing of others' goods.

Nothing has come close to this day: she needed that bit of adventure.

Criminal blood then, most probably, yes.

She wonders if Patrick's suit fits.

32

They pay no heed to your *enoughs*. You must scream
louder, with a real voice if you are to be heard. A lot
louder than that. If you are to be freed. It is not enough
to simply scream in your head. Not enough to scream in a
vacuum. It must come out, out of your mouth. A real voice.
You have learned that now.

You are cold. Old and cold. Your balls have constricted
and your member has shrunk to a shameful size. Shame. Is
this what they are after? They are here just to shame you. To
show you how shame works. What it can do. You cannot
even see them now, these spectators if that's what they are.
The light in your eyes is too bright. You look around. This
used to be home. Now it is hell. Shame. Is that their point?
Shame. To show you how it works?

The boards are cold under your feet. Your feet are
clammy. Is that sweat? It's not the sweat of endeavour, it
must be fear. Your hands are wet too. There is a tiny red
light out there. You can just about make it out. Even with
your poor eyesight. Just about. It's there. Red. Is it a sniper's?
A sniper's sight, trained on you?

That tree. Of course you have seen it before. You marched by it many times, cracking your whip. Pompous. Pontificating. And your potbelly. And your slave: Lucky. That was his name: Lucky. You never understood his speech, whatever he rattled on about. Maybe you weren't meant to. Sometimes we just aren't meant to understand things. You cannot remember the director ever explaining it to you. Lucky's speech. You didn't much care. You were more concerned with you. With yourself. Always. You cracked the whip. But it was just play, wasn't it? Just play. The serious dramas. The pantomimes too. On stage. Off stage. Just play. It was all just play. Wasn't it?

No. There was more to it. That's why you are here. They have brought you here to show you shame. They have brought you here to show you you. What you were. What you have done. What you are. You beat the side of your own head with your fists now. You are trying to hurt yourself.
Why?
Why not?
But even your fists are soft. Old man fists. Brittle. And your head is soft. You are too soft to fight. Softness cannot fight against softness.

You walk around the stage. You used to be loved. More than anything else you craved attention. And you got it. Waves of it. Tsunamis of it coming at you from the crowds. They loved you. On the TV too. They'd see you afterwards on the street. They said they knew you, and could they please have your autograph? If you wouldn't mind. Sure. Of course. My pleasure. Smile for the photographs. But they did not know you. You did not know yourself. You were hiding. And things got hidden so deep they got forgotten.

The red light does not relent. It stays on. It does not blink.

Pinter. Stoppard. Ibsen. Strindberg. Chekov. Miller. Synge. Yes, all of those. You starred! Starred! It wasn't enough. All the power. It wasn't enough. Always more. Urges. It was just a bit of fun. Play. A different time. A different tune. Play. Never meant any harm. Play. Whip. Crack. Lucky. Trousers falling down. It was all in the play. The play was the thing. Waiting. Everyone was waiting for something to happen. Everyone waiting for something. Godot. God. Their ship to come in. Comeuppance.

Out there now. Your audience. What are they waiting for? What do they want? Shame shame shame.

Your balls grow smaller. You shrink further into yourself. If you could roll everything into a ball, a hard marble say, the kind you played with as a child. And they put you in their hands and roll you off down the aisles ... never to be seen again ... rolling away ... rolling away ... to where? You have come to a stop somewhere. Every hard marble hits against a hard wall sooner or later.

You are not hard marble. You are soft and softly withering. A marshmallow held over the campfire, but held that bit too long, blackening, then melting, dripping into the flames, its sugar evaporating, its sweetness, it has no more to offer.

This is your last outing.
You are sure they will never want you again. Anyone.

They'll never take your picture again. The picture of shame? Foundoutedness.

Too late now. Too late for Lear or love.

Flies. Wanton boys. Sport.

Where are your wife and son?

You collapse to your bony knees. Hurt. Just more of it. Once it starts. Once it starts it…

Drip to the flames. Burn on the coals.

There was a boy. Yes. Admit it. Yes. There was a boy.

Go on.

More.

You are looking out at a little red light. A sniper? You can see a little red light out there. Is that the world looking on? You can see it. Barely. It can see you. Fully. Look at the whip. Yes, you remember that. Take it boys. Take it barbarians. This is your chance. Enough. Enough. Enough already. Why only watch? To show the shame? No laugh or jeer or cry. No round of applause. No sound of appraise. Enough. Enough already. That red light. Take the whip. Do it. Now. Where is your son? Where is your wife? Lydia. Lyd. Dustbin lid. You made that joke. After you'd seen *Endgame*. It was on a stage like this. You played Hamm. Yes, you played him too. Not only Pozzo. Hamm too. You were blind. You could see nothing. Your father and mother were in a dustbin. Two dustbins. And you made jokes about dustbins. Was that back in Dorset? The old days? Or when you moved to…

Your wife. Your son. Where are they? It was Christmas. It was Christmas. And now nothing but a red light, looking at you. Tiny. In the distance. Enough. Enough. Give up. Take the whip. Do what must be done. Your time has come. This is your last performance. You are naked and shrivelled and cold and sore and worried and afraid and losing. Enough already. A dreadful phrase. All you are left with. Take you away. Roast over a fire. Drip into it. The red light. The red light sees all and will show. Where do you go after this? Surely there is no place. This is the end, surely, of all places, of all plays, no stage more barren than this. Put you down. Old dog, hot in the relentless sun, choking there, unable to bark again, certainly no bite. Or string you up. That rope. Hang from that tree. Swing. Hang yourself.

Go on.

You do not move. None of you.

Three look on.

You do nothing.

Six eyes plus one red light looking and no one does anything.

Is that enough for the six eyes and the world?

Is that what was needed?

Did you get what you came here for?

None of this have you said aloud all of this has bounced around in your head bounded and rebounded none of it has come out but you can see now with your eyes and that red dot like a sniper's target aimed at you can see now that you have said none of this aloud bounced around in your head bounded and rebounded but it does not matter because you understood it anyway can read between the lines you understand all that anyway the shame the shame the guilt the shame we all of us ...

It all ends here.

You may as well just drop the curtain.

Drop the pretence.

Drop the act.

Drop your pants.

Drop dead.

Our play is ended our play is done call it *Marshmallows* have the protagonist impaled on a stick and roast him over the fire let the world see with that red light trained on you have taken it all go on and see that red light you have taken it all go on yes there was...

You remember it now...

There was a boy, yes.

There was a boy. Yes. Only ever the one. Yes. But that was enough. Yes. There was a boy, yes. There was a boy, sure. There was a boy, yes.

His name was Benjamin.

32

They stop at the gates. All three pull the naked man out of the back of the van and they kick him towards his own turf.

Ben is carrying a gun in his hand. It looks like the real thing, but can one ever be sure? He holds this gun to Charles Cunningham's temple.

"You are hardly going to do it now," says the actor. "Seems like you had your chances."

Charles does not even face his aggressors, he looks down the driveway that leads to the open door of his spectacular house. Perhaps inside this spectacular house they are calling the police, and the police are preparing sniffer dogs, helicopters. Or perhaps they are preparing words for his funeral service, giving the press information for his obituary. *One of the finest actors ever…*

How long has he been gone?

A few hours?

Days?

"You never wanted me dead, did you?" he says, still looking off to the distance, charmed by the lights of his own property; he does not care about the gun at his head. What matter now?

Ben suddenly pulls the trigger ... and from the barrel of the gun ... a flag emerges – a joke then, just a joke, and the writing on the little square of cloth one word:

Bang!

It is a lame gag. It could be something from a Christmas cracker. It was supposed to make Brick or Brac laugh their arses off – that was its original intention when Ben was making his plans, but the brothers cannot even raise a smile. They are tired now and they want to go home and lord over their loot. And they want to know the answer to Charles' question: why *didn't* they kill him when they had the chance? Why is he still alive, in front of them here like this? Bare. Barefaced. Ben has another gun. Brick knows this because he had cleaned it himself and handed it to Ben through the window of the car. The gun even came with a silencer. It would be no trouble to use it. But why didn't he? Why not? Ben opted for a lame gag instead, cop out, as if the whole thing has turned into some kind of joke. Is that what the play was all about? The shenanigans on stage. Just farce. The whole enterprise to end on a lame joke? Is that what a play is? After all the years. After all that was done. All that was said and done and ...

It doesn't sit right with the twins. They won't ask about it. They won't complain. Of course they won't. Words are never their weapons. Ben must have his reasons. He must have planned it this way for a particular purpose. But still. Still and all.

Perhaps Ben doesn't know himself. When it comes down to it. When it comes to that final ... do any of us ...

Everything seems too late now. It's in their eyes. All of them. Their tired eyes. Their deathly pallor. Their smells of a day too long, of too much done and yet, also, not enough.

The actor is back at his own gates; they have delivered him back, home, broken, but home – isn't that all that any of them wants? To be delivered back. To be delivered back home. To be somewhere you are wanted, needed.

Where *is* home? Can anyone ever really go back? And why would you?

Ben Morrigan is not laughing at his stupid gun-joke either. He's not laughing because tears are suddenly sliding down his sallow skin and his guts feel like they are being wrung, every last cell out of them, squeezed out and then throttled. He didn't expect it to go like this. Not now. Not like this. The ignominy. He's not sure how he expected any of it to go... but not like this. He just planned; and for years; he just bottled; and for years...

What does any of this mean? Can you ever really go back? And where is home anyway? What if you never had one?

Wring. Squeeze. Throttle.

Yes, his stomach is sore, as if he has been clenching it all day. Or for months maybe. Clenching. Or longer. More than months. A year. His whole body, clenched-up tight. Ever since he donned a grotesque Halloween mask and started on this play.

He holds the foolish fake gun in his foolish hand. He had made it to look so real. For years he's made everything to look so real: streets, homes, living rooms – he's built them all at some stage... for some stage.

All he wants is the curtain to drop now.

Drop it.

Drop everything.

He's fucking tired; all the acting; who is he anyway? The quiet morning one at the kitchen table, focused, intense, or the loon on the stage, anxious and antic?

Charles is not ready to face his family just yet. Naked and cold and shuddering in the sleet, to his captors he turns:

"That story about the dog, and you hitting the ball into its mouth, you know that's an old folk story, don't you? The story of Setanta. An old Irish folk story."

Charles says all this through chattering teeth. It doesn't matter now how cold he gets, he's beyond it. He's probably very sick. He's probably raging with fever. He might already be dead.

"And you know it never happened, don't you?"

Ben looks at this man's face, a face he's kept in his head for decades – it seems to have shrunken in the past few hours. Everything about the man seems to have withered away. Was that the point of it all? To see a big man wither? A big man reduced?

Why does it all feel like a let-down? Ben. The twins. It doesn't seem enough somehow. Why are there never enough happy endings? No explosions: not in this play. Christmas crackers, not firecrackers: lame. And not the crack of heads against asphalt. That's what Ben wanted to hear, wasn't it? The crack of a head against the winter ground. Well … where was it?

Ben lets tears fall, they are few but they have enough volume to scald; this is not the way, this is not the way it was supposed to be.

How *was* it all supposed to be?

"The dog. The choking dog. Did it work out for you? Is this what you wanted?"

Of course Ben knows it was an old Irish folktale. The Sisters, of course they told him; they told of so much to the unfortunate bastards. Full of stories. Full of their own theatrics.

Ben continues to cry, though he's not sure if he can say why.

The dog?

The day?

The failure?

The play?

Charles takes one last look at the three figures surrounding him. He looks out at the two vans parked there, one obviously loaded with his own stuff. His very valuable stuff. But it doesn't matter now. Nothing does. Nothing matters. And what is *valuable* anyway?

All four of them, he is sure, are as despicable as each other, as heroic and flawed as each other, and in the sleet that slants down on a Christmas night, they all are distinctly aware that they cannot distinguish between tragedy or comedy. Beckett had to glue them together: *tragicomedy*, for that play on the country road, the lonesome country road, that tree, and the light gleaming only an instant, then, naturally, night so soon, again: you couldn't have one without the other, day and night, and you couldn't separate them, tragedy and comedy.

Or good. Evil.

Charles staggers up the long driveway, the gravel hurting the soft soles of his sore feet. The broken man stumbles, but he stumbles on, mumbling to himself: *You never wanted me dead, did you? You never wanted me dead.*

Stumbling.

Mumbling.

But there is no one to hear him now, the others, the three, they have driven fast away with their own mumbling, their own wondering whether they have won or not. Fine margins. Winners. Losers.

There is nothing more any one of them can now do or say. It is far too late in the day.

What day *is* it anyway?

Still the Eve?

Or has it rolled on over to Christmas Day?

A time for giving and receiving.

Tragedy. Comedy.

Good. Evil.

Which one ever truly the victor?

Hard to say.

In the passenger seat of the van Ben closes his eyes as Brick Herbert drives, one van in front of the other, down country roads and onto suburban roads, and onto city streets: they all segue into each other, seamlessly, all sleek with rain, the whole story wet now with rain, sodden, drenched with a kind of bathos. There was never any chance of snow. Nothing magical here. No chance of that. It was never on the cards. It was always going to be grainy, grim. Ben knows that now. It was always going to be rainy and there was no chance ever of a single snowflake. You can only plan for so much.

They do not play any music in the vans. And they certainly don't listen to any Christmas songs on the radio. They let the hum of the engines lull them into some sort of winter trance. And they drive towards the end of their occasion.

As well as knowing about the impossibility of magic (beanstalks, fairy tales, snowflakes) Ben knows too that in a few days he will travel to Amsterdam to do a deal. A tall man with slanted eyes will meet him in some side-street café. The man will be wearing a sleek business suit that seems to glimmer in the weak January sun. He will drink coffee with this man, and the man will joke that Ben can smoke cannabis if he wants to – that's what most British tourists do when they arrive in the city alive with prospect, giddy with their own gumption. Ben will smile along and tell him that he's not there to see any of the sights, he's there just to do business and then get on to somewhere else. Be somewhere else. New. Anew. He wants to be somewhere new, be someone new.

And so they will do the damn deal. The suited man will be pleased with the pictures of the artefacts he is shown on the phone and Ben will be glad to be rid of it all. The horde. It won't be a fortune but it will be something. It will be substantial. If only the memories could be so easily rid.

They will shake hands after that and the man will walk away and they will never cross paths again. Ben will run his fingers through his lengthening hair. He will grow it out, long again. He might never ever leave scissors near it. He remembers one of the younger nuns saying she never wanted to cut it, that he was like Samson, maybe he needed it for his power, it held all his strength. In the Bible Samson had pulled down the pillars, but Ben had no notion of doing that. He needed his pillars. He needed to be between them. That's when he was at his strongest. And safest. But somehow Ben feels he has let them down. He can't shake that feeling. Can't shake that one off at all. Time, he supposes. It'll take time. Time to process. Time to heal. Ben might even go so far as to colour his hair a ridiculous peroxide blonde. Be someone else entirely. Put on another mask. A new persona. But he will never let anyone else run fingers through it, that's for sure. No one will be allowed get close again. Who is he anyway?

Ben will stay and finish his espresso and look at his phone. He will watch the final stage performance of Charles Cunningham, the sound off, just the decrepit figure on stage going through hellish mute motions. This act without words: it could be another Beckett outing, a moribund grasping, groping for something, a way out, an exit, an answer; Charles Cunningham staring off into the blackness, and the red recording light there, in the distance.

Ben will keep this digital file on his phone. He will probably never use it. What for? For what purpose? He will probably never delete it either. But in much the same way he let hot tears fall on the cold night outside the gates of the big house, he's not sure he will be able to say why.

In his dreams, as the van drives, Ben knows more. Not just what will happen by a canal or a shadowy side street in Amsterdam, he thinks he knows too that David will open the bags that had been left there in the Cunningham house. The suitcase. The holdalls. David will open these and find them full of fake plastic rocks. Fake plastic rocks! Just another fucking joke. The props man, sticking it to them all. Funny, isn't it? Funny. And David will rage and cry like a spoiled child and throw them around the sullied house. No one will record that.

David may perhaps be in his own flat someday, making shitty instant coffee, and pouring it into his stupid Star Wars mug, and something will strike him. A notion. Quickly he will find Ben's business card in a kitchen drawer and call the number embossed upon it. No one will ever answer that phone because … the number and the office do not exist. They never have. Like Ben Morrigan. Who? Who? David will fling the mug across the kitchen and it will hit the wall and shatter into pieces. The shards and the brown liquid will dirty the floor and that will be the only thing that makes any semblance of sense to him. A mess. A dangerous, dirty mess. He won't even bother to clean it up. He will move back in with his family and they will try to mend each other and they will try to forgive each other and they will try to understand each other, the son and the sinner and the baffled aching mother, and live with each other, they will try to live with each other and start again to love each other, if they can … but this will be all incredibly difficult, yes, incredibly so.

And they will hardly ever leave the grounds. They will just stay there. It will be more like a mausoleum than a house. It will be as if ghosts traverse the rooms there. Trapped in some glum netherworld. Too insubstantial to break their way back into this one.

34

One of the tall boys, Richard, or is it James, picks up the *sliotar* deftly with his hurley and sends it high into the sultry air, and the long-haired lad has no trouble catching it on the end of his stick and playing it back again. These are high-octane days. Days of running, sprinting. Colts they are, like young colts, hardly human at all; young muscles manic on the move, not yet fully grown but for all that unstoppable.

This could go on all day. This could go on all the livelong day. The back and forth of it, through dandelion puffs and swarms of midges and nectar-carrying bees, through the beams of the sun until the beams of the sun wane and the young bodies tire too and become weary of the day… but the back and forth of it has been made to suddenly stop. And before they know it they are marched to the central office and Sister Rose's hawk-eyes, leering over her hawk-nose, glare at them.

"I'll ask you only once more, which one of you yobbos was it?"

Their eyes fall, looking to the only carpet in the whole building. They will not speak. They will not snitch, will no way dob the other one in. They are, these three, united. The tighter you bind a band of arrows together the less chance they have of breaking. The shorter, younger one with long hair stands in the middle of the taller two, the twins. A trio. Break that.

"Right so, it'll be all three of you."

They know the drill. They do not even have to be told. Already they are loosening their belts or undrawing the strings of their shorts and lowering them.

They show no emotion.

"You know I take no pleasure in doing this lads, but I'm left with no other choice. What happened out there today is a grievous sin. One of God's beautiful creatures struck down like that."

James Herbert goes first. He shuffles the few yards to her desk and bends over it. Sister Rose reaches for her switch of birch and lashes the boy across the buttocks. Twelve times. It's always twelve. For the twelve apostles. For the months of the year. And for other reasons they cannot recall. Each lash stings and the boy's skin lets rip with an aria of pain. But he does not yell. He hides his wince, will allow neither grimace nor groan. He has hardly said a word since the day he was born; he is unlikely to start bawling now.

His twin Richard takes the second twelve, it could be an exact repeat of the first torturous scene, but too, no grumble.

And then the shorter one approaches.

"Get the hair out of your eyes."

He does as he is told. Once he was knock-kneed and nervous, but no longer. He looks at her without regret, without malice, without spite or blame, without fear, without love, without anything at all. They are just eyes, just eyes receiving light. Receiving information from the world that needs to be decoded. An upside-down world that needs correcting in the brain.

He bends across the desk. She takes her position behind him. He takes his twelve excruciating lashes. Although her old arms are tiring, she puts extra heft into these particular welts for she has a fair idea that it was his shot that did the damage. She has seen him play. She knows how talented he is with that stick – they could use him and his skills back on the old sod – and she knows that when he aims he never misses.

Like his companions before him he shows no reaction. His skin reddens and he will be sore for hours, perhaps days, but that's the way life plays.

They are dismissed from the room and they saunter out back into the sun.

Outside the building there is nothing but the sweet sound and smell of summer. Children's sing-song. Birds chirping and insects buzzing. One young girl runs to them and asks the twins to hold their skipping rope for them. The tallest boys in the home are very useful in this way, standing at either side while a line of girls take turns to rhythmically skip to their revolutions. Of course they always oblige. They never turn the little girls away. They are always there for each other. All of them. The whole army of them. The unfortunates who will never amount to anything. Bound by their hardships which have transcended to a kind of love.

The shorter boy slinks off to the side and finds a shaded area to sit in. He pulls back his curtain of hair and tucks it behind his ears. He is happy to sit here and watch the goings-on, even though his bottom bleeds and his stomach is sore from clenching and holding back tears.

He does not know at this moment what the future will hold. He has heard that a theatre group needs a young boy for a stage role. He has been recommended because he is a good-looking boy and has a certain aura about him, people are intrigued by him and attracted to him in equal measure; it is easy for him to draw people in.

He does now know if this theatre thing will be a success or not. He does not know anything at all really, he is just a young boy. He only knows that he will be able to handle his pains. And that he has two friends, and they will stick by him, and they will try to never let each other down.

He may have answers in the future, or he may find none at all. The important thing may just be the striving to find answers. Solutions to the problems that arise. But that's all for another day, another day when...

The dog has stopped barking. He has at least made that happen. That was his doing. He scans the place. The setting. The scene. He has quite a lot of control over this area. It makes him feel good, that sense of control.

Children at play is the only thing to be heard now, a cacophony of happy shrieks and mellifluous voices rising, rising and filling the cooling air. It is as if he has created this for all of them; as if he has put all the pieces in place here: the props, the people, even the shining of the sun, as if he has singlehandedly set the scene.

And the black dog has been silenced.

The boy will sleep peacefully this night. Maybe no bad dreams will come to him, for this night at least.

And the black dog has been silenced, and there is play.

It is enough.

For now, that much is enough.

Acknowledgments

and Thanks

To the three that really make things happen:

Svetlana Pironko
Maria Tirelli
Tanja Slijepčević

My sincere gratitude.

About the author

Colin O'Sullivan lives in the north of Japan with his family and works as an English teacher.

Colin O'Sullivan's first novel, *Killarney Blues*, captivated critics and readers alike and has won the prestigious Prix Mystère de la Critique in France.

His second novel, a literary dystopia called *The Starved Lover Sings*, was published in Russia to critical acclaim.

His third novel, *The Dark Manual*, is due to be made into a TV series.

O'Sullivan's short fiction and poetry have been published in various print and online anthologies and magazines.

To learn more about Colin O'Sullivan, please visit our website: www.betimesbooks.com.

Also from Betimes Books

Dimitri Bortnikov
Soul Catcher   ISBN 978-1-9161565-2-4

Fionnuala Brennan
The Painter's Women:
Goya in Light and Shade   ISBN 978-0-9929674-8-2

Hadley Colt
Permanent Fatal Error   ISBN 978-0-9926552-6-6
The Red-Handed League   ISBN 978-0-9934331-2-2

Les Edgetron
The Death of Tarpons   ISBN 978-0-9934331-4-6

Sam Hawken
La Frontera   ISBN 978-0-9926552-2-8

David Hogan
The Last Island   ISBN 978-0-9926552-1-1

Kim Hood
They All Fall Down   ISBN 978-1-9161565-1-7

Richard Kalich
   Central Park West Trilogy   ISBN 978-0-9926552-7-3
   The Assisted Living
     Facility Library   ISBN 978-0-9934331-9-1

Robert Kalich
   David Lazar   ISBN 978-1-9161565-0-0

Patricia Ketola
   Dirty Pictures   ISBN 978-0-9934331-3-9

Jackie Mallon
   Silk for the Feed Dogs   ISBN 978-0-9926552-0-4

Donald Finnaeus Mayo
   Francesca   ISBN 978-0-9926552-3-5
   The Insider's Guide to
     Betrayal   ISBN 978-0-9934331-6-0

Craig McDonald
   One True Sentence   ISBN 978-0-9926552-8-0
   Forever's Just Pretend   ISBN 978-0-9926552-9-7
   Toros & Torsos   ISBN 978-0-9929674-0-6
   Roll the Credits   ISBN 978-0-9929674-1-3
   The Great Pretender   ISBN 978-0-9929674-2-0
   The Running Kind   ISBN 978-0-9929674-3-7
   Head Games   ISBN 978-0-9929674-5-1
   Print the Legend   ISBN 978-0-9929674-7-5
   Death in the Face   ISBN 978-0-9934331-0-8
   Three Chords & the Truth   ISBN 978-0-9934331-1-5
   Borderland Noir (editor)   ISBN 978-0-9929674-9-9

Sean Moncrieff
  The Angel of the Streetlamps ISBN 978-0-9929674-6-8

Colin O'Sullivan
  Killarney Blues   ISBN 978-0-9926552-4-2
  The Starved Lover Sings   ISBN 978-0-9934331-5-3
  The Dark Manual   ISBN 978-0-9934331-7-7
  My Perfect Cousin   ISBN 978-0-9934331-8-4

Gérard Ramon
  In Love with Paris   ISBN 978-2-7466-8421-8

Kevin Stevens
  Reach the Shining River   ISBN 978-0-9926552-5-9